LEADING THE CHEERS

LEADING THE CHEERS

a novel

JUSTIN CARTWRIGHT

CARROLL & GRAF PUBLISHERS, INC.
NEW YORK

First Carroll & Graf edition 1999

Carroll & Graf Publishers, Inc.
19 West 21st Street
New York, NY 10010-6805

Library of Congress Cataloging-in-Publication Data is available.
ISBN: 0-7867-0658-9

Manufactured in the United States of America

For my brother, Tim

Author's Note

Properly, Tecumseh was the brother of the Shawnee Prophet, Tenkswatawa. Tecumseh tried to form an alliance of the Indian peoples to resist the never-ending waves of settlement. It was a hopeless task. He was killed at the Battle of Detroit in 1813, fighting at the side of the British. His body was never recovered.

I have taken many liberties with the facts. Although he bears no responsibility for this, I am grateful to Dr Charles Cleland of Michigan State University for his advice, and I have drawn on his book, *Rites of Conquest*, which details the history of Michigan's Indian bands.

Another caution: the Mide rites I describe are drawn haphazardly from a Smithsonian Bureau of Ethnology account of 1891 by W. I. Hoffmann.

I am also grateful to Katherine Tierney, of the Bay Mills Band of the Upper Peninsula of Michigan.

Nothing in this book, however, should be construed as a reliable guide to Native American practice or belief.

The Museum of Mankind in London was extremely helpful in allowing me to view artefacts, and I spent a pleasant couple of days at Monticello with Peter Hatch, Director of Gardens and William Beiswanger, Director of Restoration.

Language sets everyone the same traps: it is an immense network of easily accessible wrong turnings.

Ludwig Wittgenstein

The body supplies the immediate necessary condition of the occurrence of experiences.

A. J. Ayer

Another sign of our times, also marked by an analogous political movement, is the new importance given to the single person.

Ralph Waldo Emerson (1836)

The Indian was the representative of his ancestor or clan, an actor who performed his appointed character.

Marcel Mauss

America is a vast conspiracy to make you happy.

John Updike

Pale Eagle Speaks

I am Pale Eagle. I am the son of Red Deer and Wenonah. I was born in a cabin on the banks of the Sawgrass in the Ohio River Valley. My birth parents were John and Eliza Tucker, and I was christened John Tucker. When I was eight years old my family were killed by a band of Ottawa and I was taken away. I remember the flames of our cabin licking the night. I remember my mother being dragged from her bed. My father appeared to be peacefully asleep. I wondered why he was lying there, embracing the floor. My mother's cries were soon lost in the forest. I remember weeks of travelling by canoe, wrapped in furs. The canoe had thick black pitch markings at the stem and stern, repeated in the middle, the signs which decorated the war canoes of the Ottawa. The canoe was made of birch bark, braced by six wooden struts, and sewn together with bark thread and the skin of deer softened to make strong ties. I remember the dip of the paddles and the brushing of the water as the prow probed cleanly, on and on, through the rivers and lakes. When the canoes had to be carried, I was pushed in a sled, which had two bells hanging directly above my head. Days and nights passed. Sometimes the Ottawa would dance and sing, but mostly they spoke only sparingly, gliding down the rivers and across the snow. It was a world of sounds – the waters soughing, the snow under the runners whispering. These were the sounds of my people, the sounds of bark on water, bone on snow, wind in trees, the gentle footfall of moccasins and snowshoes.

After two or three moons I was handed over to my new mother, Wenonah, exchanged for furs. When I had learned the language of the Ojibwa, my mother told me that her son, Little Otter, had died and she longed for another son and my father Red Deer had entered the lodge and gazed upon the scrolls and fasted there, and then it had been revealed to him that Wenonah would become the mother of a pale child, with hair the colour of autumn leaves, and when they saw me with the Ottawa, they knew that I was the one, for I had russet hair and a very pale skin and they traded me for beaver and otter pelts which were sold to the Frenchman. They named me Pale Eagle, but I never forgot my English name, John Tucker, even when the fear of that night on the Sawgrass had ebbed away. The smell of the cabin burning and the sound of my mother's cries and the sight of my father embracing the deal floor, eventually became memories without substance. The smoke left my nostrils and my ears ceased to ring. I found instead a kinship with my new family, but also with the bears and the deer and the trees and rocks and water, standing or running. Red Deer said that my birth family were not far away, separated from this world only by shadows. When he thought I had sufficient understanding, Red Deer instituted a Ghost Supper so that I could speak to them and I found that they were happy in the spirit world, separated from this one only by shadows. When I knew that they were content, my mind eased. Red Deer taught me how to hunt and to set traps and where to place the nets for the whitefish and how to spear the sturgeon. I learned to make meat.

✳   ✳   ✳

And about this time I began to have visions and I would lie in the tipi sometimes for days as the spirits talked to me and Red Deer was pleased, although Wenonah tried to discourage me, fearing that I might be ill, for I was often feverish with my red hair stuck to my head as though I had plunged into the river. After some moons she too accepted that I was a jessakid. (In our language a jessakid is a shaman or medicine man.) The Great Spirit, Kitchimanitou, was conferring power on me when I lay in a trance and the Great Spirit instructed me to travel to other lodges in the lakes to learn about the Midewiwin and to study the scrolls inscribed on birch bark, that contain the lore and the music which have been passed down from the spirits to us.

At the same time Red Deer taught me to live in harmony with the animals. He taught me to pray for forgiveness when we killed the bear, our totem, begging the bear to understand the need we helpless ones had for oil and fat and warm skins. He showed me how to honour the bear, by building a lodge for him and decorating his neck with a beautiful wampum belt of shells and quills before we took the skin. If the bear — and the deer and even the sturgeon — does not wish to be killed, the hunter cannot kill him, but if he is willing, the hunter cannot fail. The great hunters of our people know the animals of the forest and they persuade them of their fitness to kill. For my people hunting is not a recreation but life, and there is no more than a shadow between life and death, and there is no barrier between the past and the present. Our world is open and shadowy and without limits. Our world stretches backwards in time and upwards to the sky and down below beneath the water.

We are actors, acting the roles the Great Spirit has given us, and these roles are the same roles as our ancestors played. I learned much in the lodges of the Midewiwin.

Yes, I am Pale Eagle of the No Ka, the Bear, totem. And I belong to the Kakinishisha clan, the sharp claws. My grandfather, White Elk, was the chief of the Bear clans and spokesman for all the clans of the peoples of the Great Lakes in their dealings with the French and the English. Our totem is a bear, standing on its hind legs, its huge paws wide, protecting us. It stands outside our lodges in the forests where we spend the fall, hunting and collecting maple syrup. All the plants of the forest are familiar to us. On the shore of the lakes are gentians and sedges and in the bogs, swamp rosemary, water lily, cotton grass, cranberry, poison sumac, spruce and cedar. In the conifer forest there is wild rose, star flower, thimbleberry, mayflower, huckleberry, bunchberry and club moss. The Great Spirit gave us these plants and these forests to use, and I learned how to make medicine; and the spirits told me how to make a medicine bundle in the shape of an otter and in it I have a hawk feather, weasel skin streamer attached to a stick inscribed with sacred signs, a miniature canoe and snowshoes, an eagle feather, a small lance and a rope of human hair. The spirits informed me what to place in my bundle and I wandered far in our country.

Our country is beautiful, utterly beautiful; it is ours to roam and it provides everything we need. The forests are the home of the deer and brown bear, the streams and rivers teem with otters and beaver and the lakes boil with sturgeon and whitefish.

The American people came flowing in their wagons from beyond the mountains and they made war because they wanted to take our lands and they drove the English to Grandmother's country. Our people were afraid because they knew that the white race is a monster who is always hungry and what he eats is land. Pontiac the great chief long ago told the English: *The Great Spirit gave us these lands and these woods and these lakes and we will part with them to no one.* But the white people did not care. They made promises, but their promises were like the smoke from our pipes, rising into the air and vanishing. They are like crayfish, unable to walk in a straight line.

And the Great Spirit said to me: On earth you will make a nation live and you shall have the power of the wind. You were named Pale Eagle because you will ride the wind. And it is true: in dreams I have flown to the upper regions and I have encountered the thunderbirds. I have roamed in the land of the giant where the thunder lives and I have listened to the spirit of the sky and smoked his pipe.

And now the spirits have told me to make a war bundle and they have told me what to put in my war bundle: a pipe in the shape of a bear's head, the feathers of swift-flying birds, a tie of bison hair, a feather headdress, a memory stick, a drum beater and a whistle made of bone.

The bison hair must be twisted into a rope for securing prisoners.

I

London

The paint on my house is so thick it looks as though it has been iced. All the houses around here are gleaming white. Many of my neighbours are in investment banking, and I think this whiteness appeals to them. White and off-white suggest deliberate restraint, hinting at reserves of character and cash which poorer, and more lurid, people do not possess. The speculators who built these houses in the early part of the last century did not build them well. The area is in a constant state of building flux, partly because of the very mobile nature of employment in the banking world, but also because every small improvement involves major reconstruction. About the time I die these houses will be approximately two hundred years old and all of them will have been re-built five or six times.

Stephanie, with whom I lived for eight years, has moved to a loft in what she calls a more real part of town. I am now living all alone. Although I sometimes miss the domestic constraints, I find myself enjoying the solitude. I have come to the conclusion that I am not a sociable person, which has made me wonder why I thought I was for so many years. But then, what is a sociable person? Somebody who can't bear to be alone, somebody who has no intellectual interests, somebody who is afraid of silence?

I am alone in my excessively white house with a wire-haired dachshund for company. He is happy too: he lies on his back as I stroke his thinly planted belly; his mouth, with the little brown cone of hair beneath it, opens and he sighs. Since Stephanie left, his behaviour has become less frantic. He no longer has to compete for my attention and he enjoys the mental release this has brought him. I remember psychology experiments which demonstrated that rats were unhinged not by the pain of electric shocks, but by uncertainty. He basks like a reptile in the warmth of my unmediated affection. Only when I take him for a walk in the Square, the biggest private gardens in London, does he display his natural excitability, straining at the leash and letting out stifled shrieks, hoping to escape. I am on the garden committee so I do not allow him to shit except in the designated area, something which he usually does neatly and quickly, backing up against a tree. Before eight in the morning we permit dog-owners to let their dogs run free in one section of the garden, although they are charged to remove the droppings to the bins provided. Sometimes rogue droppings are found. For the garden committee, the owners' carelessness provides proof of the deteriorating standards of society beyond the Square.

I had a dream about the dog last night. I was driving away in my car and he was running along the pavement trying to keep up. He ran surprisingly fast on his stumpy legs but eventually he gave up and slowed to a despairing walk. The flying ears drooped. He sat down exhausted. But the worst aspect of this dream was the look on my face as I drove. (I was outside myself, looking on.) I appeared to be brutally indifferent, like a South American dictator. My face was fleshy as though years of professional cruelty had added strips of flesh, pemmican, raw hide, to my own boyish face. My features were moist, the moisture consistent with being in a stifling car in a tight uniform in a tropical place. I had the sensation of being choked by the scrambled egg on the uniform, the copper wire, which formed the gold wreath decoration, cutting into my jowls.

The other day, as I walked down towards the Portobello Road, I saw a large, chauffeur-driven Lexus pass by. Sitting in the back, asleep, his face desperately tired, probably from a trans-Atlantic, or even trans-Pacific, flight, was my old friend and former partner, Pete Krupat. The car stopped briefly at the lights outside the Artiste Assoiffé restaurant, and he and I were only feet apart – perhaps not even two feet – but he was asleep. It was ten in the morning. His clever eyes and pinkish mouth – a mouth which had uttered charming wedding speeches, announced increased profits and performed generous sexual acts – was dragging downwards as though middle age were applying a gravitational pull. His eyes, with their quite pronounced lids, were not so much closed as shuttered for the season. He had that resigned helplessness which hospital patients and people in the thrall of religious experience have.

His face looked quite different, in fact, from my own, overbearing dream face. I pondered the connection between my dream and my chum's unguarded nap. Now that I no longer have a job, I have decided that I must open myself to the bounty which life has to offer. There are many explanations and there are many ways of living. I am, in my new situation, aware of what I have missed, but also I believe – and this is more troubling – that there must be many aspects of life's richness of which I have no inkling.

There's more to life than work, Stephanie used to say. She was right, although her reason for saying that was not strictly philosophical, more of a protest at the evident fun I had in advertising. Last year our agency, Krupat, Murray and Silas (I am Dan Silas) was bought by the Japanese group Kumishko, so releasing me into the thinner air which the unemployed breathe. My package included medical care, full pension entitlements and a lump sum which at first seemed large but now, divided by the number of years I am likely to live, seems rather small. I do still have some shares in the agency which I am proposing to sell back to them. Pete Krupat was asked to stay on: the Japanese admired his demeanour, seeing in him something substantial which they evidently did not see in me. Krupat said that the Japanese had no irony and could not understand me. 'I'm a boring fart, a plodder,' he explained generously, 'and that's why they like me.'

He is a global vice president. But a strange thing has happened: I no longer understand exactly what it was I did in advertising. I can only say that I specialised in the arts of presentation and persuasion, having seen that while many people could draw storyboards or write copy, very few could manipulate meetings. Apart from the second Tuesday of every month, the meeting of the garden committee, I no longer have meetings. I now believe that my talent was a very minor one, and extravagantly over-rewarded.

Every morning, after walking the dog, I wait for the post. Our postman, despite his vigorous life, does not look healthy. His skin is showing signs of trouble within; a tinge has spread over his cheeks, a sort of threadwork of veinous blood vessels, suggesting cardiovascular irregularities. The surface of his skin is being irrigated by diverted blood; that is my diagnosis. I would guess that the beneficial effects of walking miles every day are nullified by his daily breakfast of sausages, egg and bacon. I have seen him with his fellow postmen gathered for these huge breakfasts at Lil's Café, near the Electric Cinema. There's hardly a person left in the developed world who does not know that this sort of diet is fatal, yet Cockneys must have it. All Cockneys are unhealthy as a result. As the postman approaches the front door, the dog readies himself. He barks ferociously as the letters and circulars and junkmail cascade on to the mat and launches himself unsuccessfully upwards towards the brass flap. Sometimes I open the door and thank the postman. I half believe that a postman who knows you won't throw your mail away, which postmen with domestic problems are said to do. What I am hoping for from the post I'm not sure; a summons of some sort probably.

Yesterday just such a summons arrived, an invitation to be the key-note speaker at a reunion of Hollybush High School, Hollybush, Michigan. The reunion was to take place in the Holiday Inn on Interstate 97 at the junction with US 23, and there would be dancing to Mike and the Mellotones, who played at the Senior Prom in 1968 which was held in the old gym with the bleachers folded back. The floor was criss-crossed with the markings of the basketball court. The theme that year was Hawaiian Sunset; there were palm trees and strings of pastel-coloured light-bulbs. Mike and the Mellotones made a brief attempt to create the sumptuous, sighing, somewhat nauseous guitar sound that the Polynesians invented, but soon they gave up and played the Beatles and the Beach Boys, I think, although the music of those years has fused into a kind of Muzak in my mind. Nineteen sixty-eight was the year Bobby Kennedy was killed and of course I'll never forget that, particularly the television pictures of him lying bleeding on the floor at the back of that hall in California, strangely unmoved by the chaos around him.

The letter accompanying the invitation was from Gene Brewer, our Class President. It is clear that he has kept in pastoral touch with the class for nearly thirty years. I haven't seen any of them since my family moved back to England at the end of our senior year. The invitation was printed in that small-town fashion, in silvery ink, and decorated with a pair of palm trees leaning inwards towards the words *Grand Reunion*, lending them tropical glamour. I sniffed it to see if there was anything of the old place adhering to it. Gene's return address, in looping handwriting, in the top left-hand corner of the envelope showed that he had moved only as far as Flint, the home of General Motors, my father's employer, and also the place — I now recalled — where we had gone looking for black hookers in our junior year. We did find some once; they were frightening and contemptuous and we left chastened, although Ron Dakin swore that he went back. We greeted him for months with 'Dropped off yet, Ronnie baby?' even though we did not really believe that he had returned alone to those rancorous women with their big wet mouths.

Gene said that Gary Beaner wanted to see me again; Gary had been in and out of mental homes for many years, but was currently living with his mother, long widowed, in Holland, Michigan. He had suggested that Gene contact me. Gene said that he believed I could help Gary in his recovery. He said that Gary had important news for me, the sort of historical knowledge, I guessed, which mad people often find a burden to bear alone. He and I had been very close for the three years I was at Hollybush. His uncle owned the Music Box, an old barn converted to a dance hall on their apple farm just outside Hollybush. Gary never danced. He sometimes watched, apparently amused and distracted, but he never joined in. He said his uncle kept him too busy with the root beer concession. He was awarded a scholarship to Harvard in our senior year, the only one in the history of Hollybush High. It was there that he first had a breakdown, lying face down in the snow in front of the Widener Library saying he was learning to swim, still a requirement for all freshmen in Mrs Widener's bequest. Her son drowned on the *Titanic*.

My father was sent back to Europe to launch a new car for the Benelux countries, the GM Ranger. Later he was to say that the launch failed because of cultural misconceptions back in Flint. The Benelux public were unable to see an advantage in a car made expressly for them. Their countries were very flat — *le Pays Plat* as Jacques Brel mournfully confirmed — and people suspected that the Ranger could not climb hills. Only forty-three were sold. My father left the auto industry and applied himself to the relatively new science of marketing.

So I lost touch with my class. I was living in the world of Antonioni's *Blow Up* with a soft corona of hair on my head and velvet items in my wardrobe. After intensive private coaching I made it into Oxford to read Philosphy, Psychology and Politics. In my newly acquired vocabulary, Hollybush High seemed to have been a category error, as though I had been living by the wrong premises, and consequently drawing the wrong conclusions. Like my father, however, I retained a belief in the boxfresh character of America, a country free of monkish ignorance and superstition, as Thomas Jefferson put it. It was that ignorance which sank the Ranger.

American heroes like Jefferson, and more recent heroes like

Thomas Alvar Edison and Henry Ford, had a strong hold on my imagination. They stood for progress, a notion already being sullied by contempt for the military-industrial complex. Very little of this scepticism had reached Hollybush. In fact 'a true highlight of the senior year' (the *Redskin Yearbook*) was a visit to the Henry Ford Museum and Greenfield Village in Dearborn just outside Detroit.

In Edison's laboratory Gloria Swarthout and I listened, entranced, to the guide. He had a beard like Lincoln's, severely cut on a straight line parallel with the ground just where his lower jaw began its downward curve. He told us that in 1929 Mr Ford had persuaded Mr Edison – these 'misters' were heavy with reverence – to re-enact the moment when he had first made an electric light glow, fifty years before. Mr Ford had brought the whole laboratory, including some New Jersey earth, from Menlo Park to his open-air museum. 'Mr Edison was real happy with the reconstruction, "But Henry," he said, "there's jes one detail that ain't right." Mr Ford was kinda perturbed, ya know. "What's that, Mr Edison?" "It's ninety-nine per cent c'rect, but it was never this tidy." My, they laughed. They laughed fit to bust. Mr Ford, he was so pleased with the whole occasion that he had this chair here, where Mr Edison sat, fixed permanent to the floor in the exact spot.'

And there it was, still bearing the ghostly impression of Mr Edison's trousers, I imagined.

You can't enter into a warm relationship with European heroes in the same way. They are marmoreal or starchy, quite inaccessible. These Americans were a reproach to the old world with its feudal constraints. Standing at the exact spot (although translocated, itself a tribute to American enterprise) where electric light was first conjured from gas and glass, I saw how important Edison was to the American character. America was bright and vigorous, and Edison was directly responsible for this happy state of affairs. The electric light was an invention with profound existential consequences.

Gloria and I, pulsing like Edison's filaments, stayed behind as the party shuffled out to see where Edison had created the first commercial power station. We ducked into the glass-blowing shop (an important trade in the manufacture of light bulbs, of course) and we kissed, her tongue fluttering over my lips in what she called the 'butterfly kiss'. My hands went immediately to her very full breasts, which I was falling slightly out of love with, a churlish reaction to their old-style bounteousness and possibly to their decoy value. We caught up with the main party a few minutes later to hear the guide say, 'Everything he worked on was designed to make life safer or simpler or happier. That's why he and Mr Ford hit it off so well.'

In the grounds of Mr Ford's museum, not far from the Cape Cod Windmill and the Pioneer Log Cabin, was the Cotswold Forge, a perfectly reconstructed — from numbered stones — blacksmith's house from Gloucestershire. It was there in a small back room that I was able to get my hand, for a moment or two, into the terra incognita of Gloria's panties. I put her new laxity down to the fact that the school year was ebbing away and that she was hoping she could delay my departure by a series of tactical concessions. Also, she was aware that the tide of sexual liberation, which had inundated places like New York and Chicago, was lapping at mid Michigan, eroding the distinctions between nice girls and sluts. She was aware, because I kept telling her about it. I also suggested that we were being left behind; disingenuously I said that we didn't want to be seen as hicks.

A few years later when I was invited to a party at a genuine

Cotswold house, I had a powerful feeling of having been there before and I experienced some nostalgia for the silky moistness of that initial encounter. That mysterious and independent part of her seemed a lot more interesting, a lot more ambivalent, than her cheerleader's breasts, which I had so admired when she was urging on the Redskins, but which had now become overly familiar. The cheerleaders, captained by Karen Wardie, wore tight sweaters with an H stitched on the front. The sexual symbolism of young girls in short skirts leaping in the air and uttering shrill squeaks was not apparent to me then.

As I read Gene's note again, poised to accept the invitation, subject to placing the dog successfully, I remembered how intense the last few weeks before the senior trip to Washington, DC had become. We had moved on in the voyage of sexual discovery. Gloria had an old Studebaker that her doting father had given her. She would never get into the back seat, because there were certain girls who vaulted nimbly into the back and she had heard how they were spoken of; we made do in the front. Before the débâcle of the GM Ranger, my father was a loyal GM man and we were a GM family, always ready to defend the company's qualities, but I came to love that Studebaker with its ice-cream-cone nose. Its seats were red leather which became agitated as we did, and released an appealing smell of beeswax, applied by a previous owner. Gloria was excited by the sight of semen and would watch the mysterious eruption she set off and sometimes cup it in her hand and then she was ready to come as I, rather half heartedly by now, followed her stifled but explicit instructions, until she shrieked once sharply (just as she did when leading the cheers) and subsided into contentment, demanding from me sentiments I could barely fake. Boys of that age can be cruel; I take no pride in this. But these memories, commonplace as they are, came back strongly as I composed a fax accepting the invitation. I wondered if I could incorporate the lost ecstasy of youthful sexual encounter into my keynote speech, even as I wondered if there were words to encompass the strange feeling that I had done this before, a million times, that I was as old as the lakes and the woods outside the steamy windows of the Studebaker. The truth is that first sexual encounters bind you to the human race in ways you do not necessarily seek.

What would I talk about? My area of expertise, the selling of ideas for shifting consumer goods, now seemed trivial. Krupat's tired face, passing so close by me, told me that we had wasted our essence in this selling business. All the clever, fashionable, prize-winning things we produced – my cabinet is full of golden lions, seagulls and bears, of many denominations – all these are now as appealing as Christmas decorations in January. And I am determined not to look back more than is necessary. I'm with Henry Ford on this one: the only history that is worth a damn is the history we make today. (Although I used to believe the theory that explanations of history were the same as the explanations of science, an idea which might have appealed to Mr Ford if he had known about it.)

Yesterday, the day I received the invitation, Pete Krupat had invited me to have lunch. To demonstrate that I was still in good standing, we were to meet at the agency. I decided not to tell him about my close-up of his unguarded sleeping face. I would have a few years ago, but now a little distance had entered our relationship, because of our contrasting circumstances; instead I would take the line that everything had turned out for the best for both of us.

His office in the new building looked down on to an inner well which contained a café and a pre-war Gaggia cappuccino machine, a wonderful article I had found in a failing restaurant near the terminus in Milan and bought for the agency. It was probably legally still mine, I thought, as I watched it sending up impatient puffs of steam. I could see Pete Krupat behind the glass wall of his office. With world-weary shrugs aimed at me, he was taking a call.

'So Pete, what's it like working for the Nips?'

'We may think of them as Nips, they may look to us like Nips, but we have trained ourselves never to call them Nips. Dan, we have a small legal problem, that's what I quickly wanted to discuss before lunch.'

'What's that?'

'Stephanie has obtained an order preventing the sale of your remaining shares. She says, apparently, that you are reluctant to give her money.'

'She says in person, or her lawyer says she says?'

'Both.'

'So what are you going to do?'

He paused and composed his face. He has slightly olive features, rounded but far from emollient.

'I'm going to abide by the law. We can't buy your shares until she agrees. The Japanese don't like skeletons in the cupboard.'

'They didn't seem to mind them in Changi.'

He looked at me sorrowfully.

'Dan, Dan, things have changed around here. There is a downside, of course.'

'You speak to her, you sort it out. And then we won't mention the villa to the Nips.'

When we sold the majority of our shares, Krupat kept out of the accounts, with my connivance, the fact that a villa on the western shores of the Island of Crete, overlooking a bay of the purest blue, had been bought with the company's money. I had to admit, even as I uttered it, that this blackmail did not conform with my new desire to discover the divinity in my fellow beings, but Pete Krupat was trying to make a cheap moral point without taking into account the full complexity of human relations, particularly mine with Stephanie, to whom he had been cosying up, it seemed.

Lunch was subdued as a consequence. Krupat's face, which I knew so well, bore some recent marks. The discovery of other cultures is never without its problems; he had apparently taken a few lumps from the Japanese. There was a small crease just above his chin, and his hair, which surged backwards in the leonine nineteen-seventies style, was thinning, so that under the twinkling lights of the restaurant I could see his pink brown scalp. Until now, his hair had appeared to be of the extravagantly luxuriant variety. He had two sets of children; the second family very young. I guessed that his interest in Stephanie's welfare was prompted by familial anxieties. Jacqueline was a close friend of Stephanie and the fact that he had chosen to marry Jacqueline while I hadn't married Stephanie, probably required him to denigrate me. Stephanie and Jacqueline had been art buyers in the agency. Working in tandem they gave off an exciting promise of depravity. What I was unable or unwilling to explain to Krupat was that since I had been dismissed I was contemplating a more open and receptive relationship with life. This is not the sort of ambition which you can advertise without attracting ridicule. Our lunch proceeded haltingly.

Krupat offered to give me a lift home in his car, which was

outside thrumming expensively. The Lexus symbol was in pale gold. I told Krupat, no thanks, I was finding enjoyment in rediscovering London on foot, but he was intent on seeing a reproach in this and turned quickly to the car where the chauffeur had the door open smoothly.

I walked from Soho all through the embalmed streets of Mayfair and through Hyde Park where the leaves were beginning to loosen their grip on the trees and the ducks along the Serpentine were exhibiting seasonal restlessness. After my small victory over Krupat, I felt connected. The disconsolate trees, the milling ducks, the vapour blown wearily from the horses' nostrils as they cantered by, the blue bruised sky, the rainy squalls on the round pond, the model yachts heeling over, the freshly planted brigades of pansies, still unnaturally perfect — they were all signalling something to me, although I could not quite decipher the message. Back in Michigan I had been a fan of Emerson ever since Mr Zabruder made us learn passages from *Self-Reliance* by heart: *Trust thyself: every heart vibrates to that iron string. Accept the place the divine providence has found for you, the society of your contemporaries, the connection of events. Great men have always done so, and confided themselves childlike to the genius of their age . . .'* Although Kumishko Corp did not at first sight look much like divine providence, I was ready to accept the connection of events, the message the ducks were conveying in their quacky staccato; I was ready to trust myself.

The dog was waiting right by the door. Before I unlocked it I could hear him snuffling and whimpering excitedly. His dumb loyalty brought tears to my eyes. Unforeseen things do that to my eyes these days. I was watching a programme at two in the morning about the repatriation of pet orang-outangs to the jungle where they come from, and I found myself weeping freely. The dog licked my hand in sympathy. I carried him to the Square as a recompense for having been left alone and allowed him off the leash and into the dell for a few minutes where he pissed exuberantly on the ground cover before dashing into a thicket of spiky shrubs. When he returned quizzically, I picked him up and inverted him. I buried my face in his soft belly for a moment inhaling the meat and pastry savour of dog, and carried him back to my study where I composed my fax to Gene, saying that I would speak about Self-Reliance and asking, as if in an afterthought, whether Gloria would be coming.

Gloria Swarthout. In my memory, Gloria and Monticello are for ever joined. We had seen all the monuments and stood at the exact spot in the Capitol where you could — if I remember right — hear someone whispering fifty feet away. We had seen the little underground train which congressmen rode and we had visited one of our senators in his office. And next day we drove out to Monticello, stopping to see the Civil War battlefield of Bull Run and passing through Charlottesville to view the University of Virginia and with its great cupola, designed by Jefferson. (There was no end to this man's talents.) And the bus took us up the steep road past an old watermill to the great house which is depicted on the back of the nickel, where it looks like an observatory. We saw the tunnel under the house which the slaves used, so preserving classical order on the surface, and we inspected the extraordinary clock with interior and exterior faces. Gloria and I were lagging behind the party as it stepped out into the garden via the orangery. The grand door closed on us and there was Mr Jefferson's bed, handily equipped with his own-design device for holding books.

Gloria, perhaps responding to some historical imperative, pulled up her full, panelled skirt and slipped off her panties and we made love there, for the first time. We made love quickly, in about three minutes, and then retraced our steps through the library and front hall to the dining room, shocked and elated, where Jefferson had designed a dumb waiter which retrieved bottles of wine from the cellar below. (It wasn't fully automatic; a slave named Jupiter or Old Jupiter loaded the bottles of Bordeaux on to a sort of conveyor set into the fireplace and up they came, to the delight of his rustic pals.)

Standing in the hall underneath an Indian robe of buffalo skin, Gloria whispered that she would love me for ever. Her breath was warm from the lovemaking. And we pretended to be absorbed there in some paintings and other memorabilia, and had to knock on the windowpane to be let out into the leafy Virginian summer air, scented with dogwood, a grand tree which Jefferson called the 'Juno of our Woods'.

2

Michigan

'I know a person who went to jail for looking at one file, an FBI file. Why should they be rifling through your files? There are nine hundred at the White House. I think the trust has been violated. I think we ought to face up to it. The people see ethical problems in the White House. The President ought to say he won't pardon anybody he was involved with in business who might be implicated later on.' Rush Limbaugh goes on: 'There you have it my friends, a little summary of Bob Dole's vision.'

Limbaugh talks as I drive out on to the highway from Detroit's airport. He employs the bar-room bore's tactic of moving on to the next sentence before the previous one has settled into any meaning. His arguments are circular, but I find the bursting quality of his voice, the feeling that a sausage on the griddle is about to explode, compelling.

'I don't think Dole's attack on Bill Clinton would impact the soccer moms or the other wallflowers out there. But I'll refrain from saying any more because when I say something about anything, as you know, there's nothing left to be said. Now this is the President and his big deal about hospitals.'

Limbaugh plays the President's hoarse thin Arkansas voice talking about the closure of hospitals. I can't follow the argument.

I seem to be on the wrong road, tracking down towards the river. Appearing out of the cold, grey suburbs and thrift stores and brick-faced bars is Henry Ford's River Rouge plant which once employed a hundred thousand people. Now its smoke stacks rising out of landscapes of tangled metal make it look like a flotilla of battleships which has been mothballed or scuppered. Like those Russian ships tied up in remote ports. Only this is endless. By the time he died, Henry Ford had come to fear River Rouge. It was the biggest production line there had ever been, one of the biggest factories anyone had built, but he saw that it was eating up the small industries and crafts and making redundant that American delight in individual enterprise, and he tried to fend off these gloomy thoughts by creating Greenfield Village as a monument to what he had destroyed.

I am on Highway 95, Edsel Highway. The Edsel Ford is now a collector's piece, but in its day it was a turkey, a flop on an altogether different scale from the GM Ranger. I wonder what my father would make of the River Rouge dereliction. He saw the heyday of the automobile, and this plant – The Rouge – suggested that there were no boundaries to human imagination and invention and enterprise.

The great Jutland Fleet of River Rouge eventually gives way to small houses. Each one has some chipper little blue-collar mail-order improvement – mailbox adorned with an eagle, shingle cladding, patches of clapboard, picket fences. In the short driveways stand cars I no longer recognise, four-wheel drives, versions of

European cars and bulky Japanese people movers. Now I am passing an area where the crescent moon flag flies over shops, bakeries and mosques. There are billboards seeking the re-election to the state legislature of Marion Feinstein. Her giant picture shows her to be a full-faced woman with her hair gleaming unnaturally. She smiles out of plump, red lips. I wonder why a woman like this would want to enter the rough-house of politics, which always ends in disillusionment.

I am heading north now, through the suburbs where the workers live. Rush Limbaugh is asking if Clinton is worthy of re-election; he breaks off his exposé of Clinton's immorality, almost without drawing breath, to tell us that he personally, folks, he Rush Limbaugh finds these garden cutters to be of the finest quality. He's a fat fellow; I find it unlikely that he goes out into the garden to cut, prune and snip with his hand-forged, titanium-hardened, cutters. I see him more as a power-tool person.

I love this sprawl — the warehouses, churches, the car lots, the chapels of rest, the muffler shops, the drive-in banks, the laundromats, the liquor and discount stores. This is America's coalface, this is America's workhouse, this is America's melting pot, a ramshackle encampment of ferocious, apparently inexhaustible hopefulness. Yet suddenly I am driving through an area where half the houses are burnt out and the stores are mostly boarded up or shuttered and only a few derelicts stand on corners as though they were waiting for the transport out, which will be along soon. Now I am breaking through to the leafier parts, heralded by a few Dutch barns and stands of maize and executive estates and gift shops.

When I see French movies which deal with America, I think how self-serving they are; how they pick and choose what they like about America. And it's true that to browse through American life as Europeans do is to create a country of your imagining. I switch from Limbaugh to a country music station. When I hear Garth Brookes on Country Mix, am I hearing the same music the people in these neat farmhouses or in the trailerparks are listening to? I doubt it. When I see Oprah Winfrey and that other one, Ricki Lake, I sometimes imagine this must be some sort of parody, but the viewers may recognise issues of vital, life-enhancing importance. I don't know. All the categories are confused. In a small way I helped the process along: I encouraged people to believe that brands were spiritual entities, without knowing what a spiritual entity might look like.

I switch back to Limbaugh. He's still going on about Bill and Hillary. He is saying that Hillary used White House transport in a high-handed way. Hillary and Bill don't look to me like a happy couple, but that's not Limbaugh's point. He thinks they should be indicted rather than re-elected. He is one of the large number of people who think that other people in this country are getting away with it. In fact he seems to be the leader of those who believe that people in the East or Harvard men or the FBI or drug smugglers are getting special treatment not available to the honest. They are fixing things behind closed doors. They are hiding things from the little guy who is just trying to earn a dollar. These people, these phonies, are both dishonest and arrogant, and Bill Clinton is their standard bearer, the leader of their godless coalition: 'And this Bill Clinton, he takes the breath away. I mean didya see how he was not answering Dole's charges? He was saying, I am going to kick a field goal; no sir, he took the easy way. And Bob Dole, he's trying to get him to answer and this Clinton he just keeps on smiling. He's not going to risk a pass into the endzone, I'm telling you. He says, I can't answer that without mischaracterising the question. What does that mean? I don't know. Unless it means he can't give an honest answer. Let's take a break.'

I wonder what this is, this deep resentment. There was old Jefferson, tall stringbean Jefferson, an American *philosophe*, asking for light and rationality, and two hundred years later his people, many of whom, including Rush Limbaugh, have become very fat, the natural condition of the disaffected, spend their time torturing themselves with the imagined shenanigans of the high-ups. Some people are even saying that the fact that the man arrested for the Oklahoma bombing, Timothy McVeigh, was wearing a t-shirt with a Jefferson quotation on it — *the tree of liberty must be refreshed from time to time with the blood of patriots and tyrants* — suggests that the liberals are involved in the bombing of a Federal building.

The country opens up. I love these glimpses of the pastoral America. The perfect rows of corn, the giant harvesters working (here's a house with corn right up to the front porch), the houses so snug, placed so perfectly in the landscape; the painters they recall, Corot, Rousseau, Wedekind, all the old-world masters, put down here in the woods where the Chippewa and Ojibwa and Potawatomi and Cree and Ottawa and so on used to roam, put down and given a lick of Americanness, the kiss of special favour, now perhaps beginning to fade in this glare of discontent and unease. And the suburbs decorated for Halloween, the trees stringily encumbered with spiders and spider web, the houses with expectant pumpkin faces and the occasional cut-out skeleton dangling on the porch not too menacingly. This is the view of the world we know best, from the passing automobile, the landscape framed but moving, a moving picture. In Jane Austen the world seems to be more of a postcard, rather fixed. Physical restlessness and motion are the American inventions.

When we came back to England my father was constantly surprised and sometimes concerned as a GM executive by the lack of motion. People planned simple journeys like campaigns: where to stop with the Thermos and thin-cut sandwiches, where to let the dog out for a widdle. Where to overnight. Sometimes they consulted the Royal Automobile Club for route planners, which arrived elaborately plotted, custom made, for nervous solicitors and their families preparing to drive to Cornwall, all the way, watch out for the Exeter bypass. God knows where we would be without the restless energy which has flowed out to the world through the conduits of cartoons and movies and television.

In the Hollybush High *Redskin Yearbook* which I was examining on the plane, I saw that I was the Senior Banquet Speaker. What did I talk about? I have no idea. The book is filled with valedictory notes, which I read again. It is well known that memory is a tricky business; now it is thought that memory is not like a series of dusty, yellowing filing cards which the brain has to retrieve, but a reconstruction of the events or emotions of the time, completely afresh. But even so, I was surprised that I couldn't remember half the people who wrote in my yearbook: 'You are the greatest guy I have ever met, with a personality to match. I will never forget you.' 'You've got to admit that we had some pretty great times together. PS watch the puss.' And Mary wrote: 'Going with you was the greatest experience of my life.' What does this mean and who was she? I don't remember.

I pass the turn-off to Pontiac. And now I remember something very clearly, the words of Chief Pontiac: *I stand in the path you travel until morning.* Chief Pontiac stood in the path of the English for a while, but it was hopeless. I felt guilty on behalf of the English when we read these words. The chief himself became the figurehead of a car; his bony face was aerodynamically restyled to suit this role.

I stand in the path you travel until morning.

Morning came fast for Chief Pontiac. You couldn't stand in the path of this juggernaut, something entirely new in history. Where the Rouge plant is, Potawatomi made delicately shaped birch bark canoes and grew Indian corn. I learned this, with Gloria at my side, on an Easter field trip to Cranbrooke. At Hollybush we took information on board in a democratic, communal fashion, grouped with notebooks and pencils around visual aids. Even then I was harbouring information which was to be useful in my later life, and perhaps this is the problem, that I have forgotten what was of no use.

The leaves are preparing their autumn show now. The trees hereabouts are not as gaudily rich in colour as in New England, but they don't lag far behind. Whole hillsides, exposed to cold winds, are already taking on the chilblain red of fall. This colour runs down into the valleys, but down there it dies and you see the green bunting of summer still hung defiantly.

'What's there to say? You're a doll and I really enjoyed knowing you. Remember the boatride? Karen.' I don't remember the boatride, but I do remember Karen. Like Gloria, she was a cheerleader; she had a thin fringe which was teased into straight sprigs of hair over her forehead, like the tassels horses wear in fly-plagued countries. We had danced together at the Music Box while her boyfriend was away at college. I talked about books, as a prelude to a walk in the orchard. (Books in those days could be deployed in the cause of eroticism.) Her face became shiny.

She made it clear that I was a stopgap, and I must never tell Donny or he would kill her, and maybe me as well. She kissed with frightening intensity. There was a very clear ranking of the girls, and Karen stood right at the top, with Gloria second by some distance.

The fierceness of the winters. Fishing through ice four feet thick. I remember walking early one morning and finding Squaw Lake frozen with the ice still clear so that as we skated we could see through to the waterweed and sand and rocks below. In that lake Ed Preston's father drowned one night. He was a DJ at a local radio station, WJK. He fell off a raft, drunk. Ed was not particularly upset. Perhaps kids are a lot more resilient than adults like to believe. Adults fear for children, but their fears seem to seep out of the cracks in their own faltering lives. Ed and I skated that day without a qualm over the spot where his father had drowned only a month or two before. The lake was a glass-topped coffin. In my eyes his father's death had conferred distinction on Ed. Ed also wanted to be a DJ. He was a thin boy with dark but lonely hairs on his upper lip.

The trees and the glimpses of lakes — Michigan has countless numbers of lakes — speak to me of the exhilaration of driving the highways of America. I am elated to be rolling along, past those undercoating shops and factory outlets and computer stores and grain elevators and hunting suppliers, all interspersed with the patches of fields and swathes of wild hillside, which are committing bloody suicide, shocked into this beauty; at night the ice is forming a diffident *granita* on the lake shores, but soon you could wake up and find the whole lake roofed with ice thick as a barn door and growing thicker. I have always been intrigued by ice; Stephanie and I skied the Vallée Blanche in Chamonix and the guide said that there were fish in the depths of the glacier. This was a local joke which maybe didn't translate well, but we chuckled ingratiatingly as you do when talking to French ski guides and restaurateurs. The ice, thousands of years old, contained mysterious pools of iris blue and I could easily imagine fish in there, and much more as well. And also I think now of the boyish pleasure of jumping into iced puddles or lifting whole disks of ice from buckets. Where did the ice come from, so perfect, I wondered?

All the people I have forgotten are there somewhere, hidden away like the fish in glaciers. I'm open to discovering the immense fraternity (and sorority) of humankind.

Detroit and its satellites are far behind. The radio says that Dr Kervorkian is planning another mercy killing for the weekend. I have seen a picture of him in a little pork-pie hat and he doesn't look like the angel of mercy. A whiff of the harsh regime sanatorium clings to him. Despite his old-world appearance, he seems to have taken up a very contemporary stance: he has adopted the single interest. He drives around Michigan with bottles of potassium chloride and cylinders of carbon monoxide. He calls his mission 'medicide'. He has helped kill forty people. This weekend's patient has Lou Gehrig's Disease.

I pass a field of mysteriously unpicked corn, the tassels of the cobs waving and undulating gracefully. The editor of the *Flint Journal* comes on the radio. He proclaims the revival of Flint. 'We've had our bad times, sure we have, but now we're on the way up. Michael Moore did no good for this county, but there was a lesson to be learned and we learned it.' He gives a quick history of the rise and fall and rise again of Genessee County, once the richest in the whole Midwest. While I have been away, it seems the place has been through a complete historical cycle. My classmates have slumped and are now on the way up. When they wrote in my yearbook they were all freshly minted and brimming with confidence.

'Dan ole buddy, I didn't think you were going to make it sober on the senior trip, but miracles do happen.' 'Danny, you know what old Thomas Jefferson said, We hold these truths to be self-evident, anyone who gets locked up with Gloria is not created dumb. Your pal, Ron.' I had foolishly confided our adventure to him. Foolishly, because reputation was believed to be a precious commodity then, and girls' reputations were more fragile and more easily lost. Ron, of course, had boasted of his experience with the black hookers, so I had something on him to keep him quiet. In the yearbook Ron Dakin has large eyebrows and a long, thin face, a face which is unmistakably American in the way that American faces, made from so many bits and pieces, surprisingly often are. It's a mystery how an archetype can emerge from this genetic bran tub. And there, in regular and sober handwriting, was a message from Gary Beaner: 'A friend may well be reckoned the masterpiece of nature as Ralph Waldo Emerson said. Your friend, always, Gary.'

My friend Gary who was practising his swimming in Harvard Yard in the spring of 1969 on the very day University Hall was occupied by students protesting about military recruitment on campus. And now he wants to see me again, and perhaps this is why I am really here among the winter-ravaged cornfields and the chafed woods, to hear what Gary has to tell me about the connection of events. Gary is the only one whose voice I can recall clearly. It had a slightly hollow quality, like someone speaking in a cave or a public lavatory. I can hear him saying 'Waldo', sonorously. We thought Waldo was a knickerbocker name.

Leading the Cheers

I sail past a little development of off-the-shelf ranch homes. Each one has a carport on thin poles, clustered as if for reassurance around what must have been the original farmhouse, which sits back a little, jostled by these neat fakes, its grey and green shingled and gabled roof, rising above them. When we lived here it never occurred to me to wonder how these perfect old houses evolved from the minds of the mass of German, Polish, Scandinavian and Scottish immigrants. What guided them? How did they develop this distinctive look? Now I pass a Greek revival house, standing by its own small lake, a little temple. There were plenty of them in Hollybush. Gloria's parents had one, just behind the fire station, overlooking the cemetery where flags had sprouted as if the deaths in Vietnam had sent underground tendrils to this commodious graveyard. Now I remember that two of the graves were of boys who had been at Hollybush High only three years earlier.

Here's America sliding by my window. What convulsions it's been through. When I left, a new country was emerging; the angry children were beginning to change everything. In some places, though not Hollybush, they had done that already. But even in Hollybush there were plenty of armchair Viet Cong supporters who chanted 'Ho, Ho, Ho, Chi Minh . . .' and some of us said, 'Hey, hey, LBJ, how many kids did you kill today?' Ron Dakin, with his flat-top, was one. In the little brochure Gene has had printed for the reunion, he is described as 'a realtor in Lake Tahoe, whose prize possession is a giant redwood hot-tub. Passing cheerleaders always welcome.'

Gloria thought that some of the female protesters were losing their femininity. For myself, I was protesting not so much at the incineration of children with napalm but at Gloria's already

33

outdated, heavy-breasted femininity, which was standing in the way of a fuller sexual relationship. Also it was obvious to me that the sophisticated people were very thin. I tried to tell her about Abbie Hoffman's manifesto, 'We believe that people should fuck all the time, any time, whoever they want.' What carried me far in advertising was a glib up-to-dateness, and its roots obviously go back a long way. It is this cheapness which I am endeavouring to slough off. I will avail myself, without cynicism, of the offer to buy a commemorative brick from the old high school, which stood like a cross between a warehouse and a unitarian church among the red maples that lined Seminary Road: 'Each brick will be laminated and inscribed with a commemorative, non-corrosive brass plate, bearing the legend Reunion, Class of 1968, Hollybush High School.'

I have been to America many times, to Phoenix or to Los Angeles, to New York, to Dallas and to Florida, for the meetings required to sell brands worldwide and for film and photographic shoots, but my careless neglect of this America gliding by is making me feel guilty, like remembering some forgotten error of judgement — *the remorse which inflicts some shooting pain*, in Emerson's words. In Washington to discuss a political advertising contract, I saw Maya Young Lin's monument, a granite tomb capping off the suppressed buzzing of the dead. I now realise with pain that I hadn't looked for the names of Edwin Lynebracher and Joe Alvesteffer, Jim's older brother. I hadn't remembered that two of the dead commemorated there, whose bee-anthem I could faintly discern from within, were from Hollybush. While Watergate was happening and OJ Simpson was being tried and Oklahoma bombed, it had never occurred to me to wonder what they were thinking in Hollybush. Maybe I was blotting out my past, as provincials do, in my haste to get to where the action was. Back then I thought the action was in London. What happened in Genessee County simply had no meaning in the heady Fulham Road, where nobody had heard of Michigan, no more than they had heard of Bosnia or Croatia. Like everybody else, I made my own paste-up America from television programmes and magazine articles and films like *The Deerhunter*.

But now I remember that Lynebacher and Alvesteffer were deerhunters. We all were, as a matter of fact. We headed up to Houghton Lake as the hunting season opened, dressed to kill in red checks and double-lined boots and caps with earflaps, carrying cheap East European rifles. I remember the oily softness of the deer and their still optimistic eyes as we tied them on the hood of the Pontiac. This had to be done quickly before the deer stiffened in the intense cold and the spindly but tough legs refused to bend. And it was at the Bear's Den on the edge of the frozen lake that I first danced with Gloria and she quickly and automatically clamped her warm, soft breasts against my skinny chest. *Cheerleaders' breasts*, I congratulated myself, as if these had some special quality. The next day I saw a bear and ran. It should have been hibernating, but instead it was investigating the trash cans outside the cabin we rented with the Lock family. We slept in bunks around a pot-bellied stove.

I didn't look for Alvesteffer and Lynebracher on the memorial and it is an omission which Stephanie would be quick to tell me was in character. Stephanie said that I was refusing to marry her and declining to do what normal decent people do — people like Jacqueline and Pete — because I was too selfish. *Ordinary* people, she said with heavy emphasis, *who you despise*. Also, I refused to see anything which was not of direct use to me. It's true that I have tried to avoid people who live in deep blandness, pleading family to excuse their timidity. But now I have come to think that my own imagined distinction (and prosperity) have been bought cheap, an accident of time and place. If I had stayed in Hollybush I might be . . . I struggle to think of a profession I could have taken up. Perhaps I would be the editor of the *Flint Journal*, boosting the local economy. Would I have left anyway, had my father not been called back to England?

I could have explained to Stephanie that by accepting this invitation to be the keynote speaker, I was, in case she hadn't noticed, putting myself in touch with ordinary people. And she would have said, how do you know they are ordinary? And I would have said, you used the phrase, ordinary people, I was just picking up on that. And she would have said, don't be too literal, you know what I mean, I mean your fundamental contempt for people you don't think are as interesting as you are, which you're not by the way. And I would have said, one of the essentials for an adult conversation is the ability not to confuse the categories, and she would have said, we all know you were at Oxford and scored a third, but that doesn't mean you understand anything important or human, never mind your fucking categories. And I would have looked at those little lines around the too-bright, too-moist eyes, and stopped myself from saying anything too cruel but what I could have said was, you were a beautiful, blithe airhead who fucked like a snake, and now you are turning into just one more embittered, health-obsessed madwoman and by marrying you I will not end the process but merely accelerate it.

And these thoughts, instead of depressing me, instead of turning my mind to Stephanie's attempts to seize my money, as if some of my emotional property will stick to this money, cause me a certain elation despite the many, and irreconcilable, contradictions in my position.

Huge snowflakes are falling now. These snowflakes, as big as handkerchiefs, are aggregating fast, so that the darkening sky is becoming a solid, soiled sheet of linen. The snow is so thick that all I can see are tail-lights and a few yards of white highway. The hotel is suddenly signposted in the snow, and I make a last minute turn-off in front of a huge truck which sets up a raucous honking; the derisive tympany blows back with the blizzard as the truck thunders on towards Bay City.

The hotel is built round a large atrium, thinly decorated with isolated groups of chairs and trees in pots separated by free-standing partitions, like stands at a trade fair. In one corner of this huge, unnecessary, space is the New England Coffee Shop, and across from it is the Fisherman's Wharf Restaurant. *(When we're closed, we're out catchin' 'em.)* Outside the coffee shop a tall man dressed as a clown is holding some balloons decorated with spiders' webs and bats; beside him is a cylinder of helium. Over in a corner, at the entrance to the recreation center, is a small grove of banana and ficus trees. There is a smell of chlorine from there, and I can hear children's voices. Swimming pools cause children to shout with glee, and my spirits rise.

My room, too, is huge, opening on to the atrium at one end. Here in the Mennen Suite, the reunion is taking place. The television offers adult movies. I watch three free five-minute samples. By the third I recognise one of the male actors, whose facial agony and intensity suggest that acting sex (if he is acting) is painful and physically demanding. On another channel I see John Cleese in an ancient Monty Python routine doing the silly walk. When Gloria was babysitting at the Locks, we used to watch *Bonanza* on their huge, chunky TV set, which looked like a cocktail cabinet until you opened the doors. We both admired it.

It's only about nine o'clock here, but back home it's three in the morning. I hope that the dog is happy with my mother. I decide to make a start on my speech.

'Friends, former classmates, I want to talk tonight of something I first learned at Hollybush High School, the connectedness of events. Something which that great American Ralph Waldo Emerson communicated to us, via our home-room teacher, Mr Zabruder. Emerson also told us that friendship was the masterwork of humanity. When Gene was kind enough to contact me in London, England, having read by chance an article I wrote in *Accounting Age* about Global Advertising, I pondered the ideas of friendship and connectedness.

'For those of you – probably the majority of you – who do not know, my family who were originally from England, returned to London in 1968 when my father was appointed to a senior developmental post with General Motors in Britain. I enrolled at Oxford University and embarked on a career in advertising in 1975. Six years later I founded, with my partner Peter Krupat, an advertising agency, and earlier this year we sold a majority of our shares to a Japanese advertising group. The time since college has passed in a flash, and I find myself now older, perhaps a little wiser, wondering where more than twenty-five years have gone. And now I feel a deep regret that I never once in that time came back to Hollybush, where I was so happy and where I had so many good friends, a number of whom are here this evening. I hope that by coming here tonight I can make amends and re-establish some connections.

'Studying our yearbook and the personal details which Gene has so thoughtfully provided, I see that our class has travelled the world, mainly in the Services, had children (even two grand-children), and entered a variety of trades and professions, and suffered a fair amount of personal happiness and tragedy. It is amazing to me, however, that so many of our class should be alive and well and living still in Genessee County.'

But wait, am I being a little bit glib here? How can I explain my profound lack of interest, if I claim I was so happy here? How do I get around the fact that I had moved on without a backward glance, that Hollybush did not enter my plans? Stephanie makes it sound as though there is something calculated in my life; instead I see instead a sort of pitiable anxiety to be in the action. The reason I am here in this cheerless hotel room writing a speech is because I am now keen to open myself to random influences. I want the trade winds to blow me where they will. But I don't imagine my audience would be pleased to be told that they are part of an experiment of a personal and indulgent nature.

'I feel a deep regret that I never once came back to Hollybush High School where I was so happy. I could explain that by saying that I was focusing so intently on my career goals that I lost sight of what was important and that was friendship. While I was achieving some success, I lost sight of the connectedness of events. But now I remember with great clarity Emerson's words: *Trust thyself; every heart vibrates to that iron string. Accept the place the divine providence has found for you, the society of our contemporaries, the connection of events.* So

I am not going to agonise over my absence; instead I am going to accept the connection of events, the circumstances which have brought me back at last to the society of my contemporaries with simple gratitude. I am thinking of buying a summer place here on a lake, for a start.'

(I have thought about it, vaguely, but the truth is that if I were going to live the American pastoral, it would be on Martha's Vineyard, with Alan Dershowitz and Carly Simon.)

'But no realtors need contact me just yet – I see we have at least three in our class. Now, I know we all want to get back to Mike and the Mellotones, but before we do so, could I say, looking back to nineteen sixty-eight, when we were young, no more than children really, I see that the years which have passed have produced profound changes in our lives. And this great country, which nurtured all of us, has not been left untouched. I think it is here that the great issues of our times, feminism, race, individual responsibility, you name it – have been played out first. America, my friends, my classmates, is the most powerful nation that has ever existed on this earth – the whole of England could fit comfortably into Wisconsin – and America has become not so much a country as a world. This has been the American century. In some respects this has been disturbing. But I like to believe in all the years I have been away, that in Hollybush where we were all kids, the true America was living on, the true America on whose values this country was built, and those values, like those of my boyhood heroes Thomas Jefferson and Thomas Alva Edison, must continue to be the basis of a great society. So in conclusion, let me say that from where I was, I saw little Hollybush here in Michigan as a vital link in the great web of connectedness which, as Mr Zabruder, Emerson's spokesman here on earth used to tell us, forms the basis of all human life. I thank you for the honour of being asked to be your keynote speaker tonight. Thank you.'

Outside my window the giant snowflakes have not abated; they float down into the lighted carpark, obscuring the outlines of the cars, so that they are now like dough left to rise before baking.

3

Hollybush. Population 11,000.

I enter the town past the sawmill, which has now become a health shop and picture gallery. The sawmill was owned by Gloria's uncle. The sidewalks in the old residential areas near the cemetery are set between rows of red maples. The snow has been shovelled and nudged aside in a way which I think of as American: the work has been done quickly, efficiently to some plan so that there are neat snow banks beneath the trees. I drive around on this crisp Saturday past the fire station, where the kids have set up a charity Halloween car wash. The fire trucks are gleaming in there, authentic works of art, a backdrop to the busy washing and buffing which is going on. The kids are wearing green and blue parkas and pale fleeces or long hooded Michigan sweatshirts and caps. In the winter we used to wear thick chequered shirts and hats with earflaps. Our clothes suggested that we were ready for the outdoors, for farming or hunting, whereas these kids are dressed for glamorous sports. In Mott Street, where the Farmers' Mart used to stand, I see a Gap and a Footlocker. At first sight Main looks much the same, with its cluster of competitive churches, an estate agent, Ansbachers, with mullioned windows stands next to an adult video shop and I cannot remember what was there before. The old drugstore, Schwindell's, has had a

43

facelift, and there is a patio outside decorated with a sculpture of a porpoise.

As Gene warned in his newsletter, the high school has gone, moved from the middle of town where it had crouched, flat roofed and plain, behind the original Victorian school building of red bricks which formed a deceptively imposing entrance. These bricks are now available as souvenirs.

Movies have been made and books written about reunions because they are particularly charged. You are invited, almost obliged, to consider the quirks of memory. Other people similarly have a duty to rummage in the past, and the licence to reminisce, so freely handed around in this way, is not always welcome. What did I read somewhere, after twenty-five years the class nerd is still the class nerd? Reunions confront you with your youthful self, and that can be nerve-racking, because your contemporaries take no account of the intervening years and the efforts you have made to become something different. They remember you at your most awkward and unformed and they take delight in reminding you of it. As I pass a car lot, wondering what was there before, it occurs to me that it must be even worse for those school heroes whose lives have trailed away into failure and bitterness from a high point at the age of seventeen or eighteen. At that age you are judged by standards as evanescent as teenage love affairs.

Driving out towards Squaw Lake I see the new high school, out where there used to be a dairy and some scrubby woods of black willow. I miss the turn-off to our old house, because there is a development of four ranch houses set in big plots of perhaps an acre. This was a swampy field where I once managed to shoot a pheasant as it became airborne, screeching. There was a lot of shooting and fishing and hunting of deer.

But the turn-off is still there and the overgrown lane down to the lake is even more overgrown than I remember. Our double-storey clapboard house, built about 1920, is smartly painted, the frames of the windows picked out in pale green. From the gate I can see the window of my room which looked back over the yard. There is a fancy mailbox in the shape of a mallard with the name Alvesteffer beneath it. I get a glimpse of the lake, not yet frozen. I wonder if I should walk in and explain that I used to live there, and that I have lived in England all my adult life – hence the accent – and see if I am invited in to inspect my old bedroom. Jim Alvesteffer was in my class. After a few minutes I realise that there is no one there. The snow is undisturbed. So I walk down the uncleared driveway, feeling the cold snow crunch under the feet. This fresh Michigan snow makes a distinct noise of protest when you walk on it. The storm windows, with which my father made much expatriate-in-the-wilderness play, are not yet up, I notice critically. In the front of the house the snow lies on the grass, two feet deep. The dock, a ledge of snow, pushes out into the lake. An aluminium dinghy is still tied there, bobbing on the thickening water. Next door, where Ed Preston lived, somebody is watching me from the picture window. I wave airily and the face moves away. The lake is bigger than I remember, which goes against the accepted rules of memory, which dictate that everything remembered is smaller in reality. I have forgotten, obviously, that it extends off to the right, north-east in a huge arc. We lived here for three years, and I learned to drive and to swim and to handle a boat. My father loved the familiarity our neighbours had with tractor mowers and gas barbecues and power tools and outboard engines. Their large garages were full of them. To him, they were evidence that Americans lived in this world. Newness to them was attractive: the new models that my father was helping to launch at GM each year were discussed in detail, with reverence. My mother said that newness was a 'palliative' for Americans, but the word itself, whatever it meant, seemed to me rather old-world and smug.

On the other side of the lake the houses have shuffled a little closer together. After Kenly in Flint, this lake was where the executives from General Motors and Fisher chose to live. I wonder if there could have been a colour bar in operation around here, because our school was completely white. We were intimidated by the high schools from Flint where the black boys, who were unfairly tall and athletic, beat us at every sport. Sometimes we tried to speak like them, with a hint of Southern lushness in the voice. This morning, turning out of the hotel, I almost ran into a black woman in a Toyota, and she rolled down her window and said, 'Yo gonna have akseden, yo drive like that.' I apologised and said I was a visitor, and she smiled indulgently: 'You take it easy, y'hear.' But there it was, that profligacy with the consonants. In fact all over America black people are consolidating their language into a dialect.

The house on the lake does not produce any warmth of feeling. Instead I feel a certain detachment about the remembered details – the basketball hoop over the garage doors, the small window down to the cellar, the summerhouse at the edge of the lake – as though my few years here had been experienced by someone who had recounted them to me in detail. There is a conundrum of philosophy, the problem of establishing for certain that my experiences are definitely my own. I thought at the time I was trying to write an essay about it, that this was the sort of amusing but meaningless puzzle teachers of philosophy occupied themselves with over a glass of sherry, but now I have the strong feeling that it wasn't me who lived here at all. Of course it was my body – the body supplies the necessary vehicle – but were they my experiences? I feel cheered by this interesting question as I stamp through the snow to the summerhouse. There in the snow-reflected light is a hammock of woven string. And in that summerhouse we used to drink home-made lemonade. My sister Belinda, now a senior person in the Samaritans in Bristol (these support industries are growing), used to play her Beatles records here. She believed George Harrison had hidden depths. Belinda brings to the task of being a Samaritan a serenity which she has always possessed, as though what is happening here and now is faintly amusing. She shared this quality with my mother, who found my father's infatuation with newness endearing. He would try to explain to her the aerodynamics of the new Firebird and she would smile as though he were talking about a remote tribe he had just read about in *National Geographic*. Her inviolability irked him, I think.

'Do you care about what I do all day?' he once asked her.

'Of course, dear, as long as you are happy.'

Belinda was at the University of Michigan at Ann Arbor. She thought cheerleading ridiculous, and when Gloria came to our house she would talk to her in a deliberate and kindly fashion, as if she were not well. Gloria once told me that she had found herself 'babbling uncontrollably whenever I see your sister, like I've got to justify myself or something'. Now people who are planning to jump off the Clifton Suspension Bridge or stick their heads in the oven have the same feeling about my sister.

Unlike me, she always knew that her true home was back in England with the Beatles, and she treated Hollybush as a temporary resting place. If I talk to her now about our time in America she speaks of it as if it were an amusing interlude amongst half-conscious people.

'Dan,' she said when I told her I was going, 'we were there. We lived in the middle of nature amongst amiable morons. It was boring. Yes it was America, but unfortunately it was the kind of America nobody knows or cares about.'

This has been the American century and Hollybush, no less than any other place, is a constituent part of that uncontainable phenomenon. Everything is connected.

I walk through deep snow down towards the lake. My feet are sinking through the light crust. I can't shake the feeling that a gulf has opened up between me and the boy who played basketball here, and skated there, and read *Playboy* up there in the bedroom, and practised throwing the football to Ed on the front lawn; our lawn and theirs merged in front of our houses.

Down by the lake shore, however, the water itself unexpectedly stirs my memory sharply. The edges are beginning to freeze half heartedly, and the water has a colour, a sort of blue vegetable tinge like those fancy lettuces, a colour that comes back to me almost as painfully as the pang of jealousy. It's just water. But when I put my hand in it and drink the taste of vegetable decay and minerals, the taste of lake water also comes back as though it's been my daily tipple.

'Hello there,' says a voice.

I stand up, as casually as a man can who has been kneeling in snow drinking lake water. I turn and see a stout man in a blue woollen fleece standing near the house.

'Hello,' I say, 'excuse me, but I used to live here once.'

'That's okay, the lake water's still free. About the only damn thing that is,' he says. 'The Alvesteffers are away, and I wondered what you was doin'.'

'Do you live there?' I asked gesturing, 'in the Webb house?'

'That's the Robinsons'. No, I'm just keepin' an eye out for the place. I'm Wally Kapinsky. Property maintenance. Are you British?'

As he approaches, stepping through the snow in shin-length double-laced boots, I see that he has a broad Slavic face, common around here, the eye sockets pronounced and widely spaced and the eyes themselves a faded blue, the colour of old denim.

'Yeah. My dad was with GM back in the sixties. This was our home for three years. Dan Silas is my name.'

'Okay.'

He's looking at me closely.

'You said this is the Alvesteffer home. There were two Alvesteffers at Hollybush with me.'

'This here's Jim Alvesteffer. He lives mostly down in Bloomfield Hills now. He's with Ford. His brother Joe died out in Nam.'

'Were you at Hollybush? Your name rings a bell,' I ask him.

'Ding dong. I was thinking the same thing. But you know I was one of the dumbklutzes doing metal work and shop. I was in the class of sixty-seven.'

'I remember you. You were on the track team.'

'I was. Pole vault. And you used to run the hundred and the two-twenty. Skinny little bastard. What in hell are you doin' back here?'

'I've come to be the keynote speaker at the reunion of our class.'

'Classa sixty-eight. Jesus, what a bunch of assholes. Present company excepted. Of course.'

'What's wrong with them?'

'What's wrong with them? Shit, what's right with them? That's the question right there. Tell me, Dan, why were you drinkin' lake water? Or were you kneeling down to take a piss?'

'No, I was just trying to remember how it tasted.'

'You'll fit right in. Classa sixty-eight, holy shit. Wing ding. Take it easy now.'

He leaves me to my private communion and heads back through the snow, rolling slightly. But then he stops.

'Dan, you're the one who screwed that Gloria Swarthout in ole Thomas Jefferson's bed, am I right?'

The broad face, abraded by the weather, by outdoor work, is a drunk's face I see, the features slightly out of line, as though below the surface alcohol produces this rearrangement, the way tree roots can move paving stones.

'Me?'

'You're the one.'

I can hear him muttering to himself and laughing as he replays our conversation: 'Jee-ziz, I don't know.'

He has a pick-up parked near the gate, where the snow is clear, just behind my rental car. And this is another thing I remember: handymen, plumbers, mechanics have these big colourful extravagantly equipped vehicles, the blue-collar workshop on wheels. My father told me that this, too, was an example of why America was successful: ordinary people had no inhibitions – he may have said hang-ups, the language was changing – about entering the practical world. Back home, he said, the working class was still deferential and constrained.

Wally gives me a wave as he leaves.

'You're the one,' he points his fingers at me as if he is taking aim with a pistol and the pick-up roars its way out along the lake.

How does he know about Gloria and Jefferson's bed? I see that my recollection of Hollybush is not mine alone. Far from it. Meeting Wally, I see now that maybe I have made a mistake in assuming that my recollection of those days was going to be the definitive one. And I wonder what Wally meant about the class of sixty-eight? You couldn't be sure if he meant anything special, because the guys who took shop were temperamentally inclined to sneer. (They were the sort of people who find their prophet in Rush Limbaugh, I would guess.) While they were learning to do useful things with welding machines and jig cutters, preparing themselves for a life on the assembly line, they saw the prettiest girls — incredibly — teaming up with the country-club boys who, like me, studied French and drama and so on, while they, the real men, had to make do with the big-haired and promiscuous girls who would end up as trailer trash or waitresses. I don't know this for sure of course, but I am confident I have the general picture.

Out on the lake, a dinghy with an outboard is towing in a line of Indian-style canoes. The lake is shining palely, its nickel surface disturbed by a breeze I can't feel here on shore. I sip the water again, and dread, as I did then, the coming winter.

I drive back into town feeling a little uneasy, and stop at Schwindell's for a sandwich and a cup of coffee, looking for some comfort. Schwindell's used to be a regular drugstore with a soda fountain and a section selling medicines and plasters and french letters, if you were brave enough to ask. Now it serves charred chicken breasts and Italian bread with a fat-reduced dressing at round tables. The booths and the counter with the little round stools have gone. Where the pharmacist reigned, there is now a gift section selling herb teas and crafts. You can choose from a range of *Seattle-style lattes and cappuccinos*, with additional flavourings including hazelnut, vanilla and almond, all at 50c. These bottles stand importantly behind the coffee machine.

The three waitresses are all Oriental, two Chinese and an Indian, but they are American in unmistakable ways too. Not just in the way the Indian girl says, 'Hi, I'm Smeeta, and I'll be your waitress,' in unironic greeting, but in their bearing: they have a teenage confidence, a barely concealed impatience. Life has placed no mark on their faces and their eyes see no obstacles. In London kids of this age, by their protective magical dress, suggest an awareness of what's coming their way. If I tell these girls that I am the proprietor of an antique cappuccino machine, made in Torino, surmounted by a hand-cast bronze eagle, which passes trickles of coffee of silky delicacy, they will smile and say, 'That sounds real neat,' in that sceptical way, the inflection rising, without having any curiosity about what such a thing could be.

Our home-room teacher, Mr Zabruder, the Emerson buff, used to eat a double cheeseburger and drink a chocolate malted milk here every lunch hour and then come back for the lunch line. He was, he once said, naturally heavy-set; it ran in his family. Now it seems he may have been right: obesity has its own gene. I take a copy of the *Flint Journal* and read about Timothy McVeigh. Much is made of the Jefferson quote here too: 'The tree of liberty must be refreshed from time to time with the blood of martyrs, which is its natural manure.' They seem to have left out the blood of tyrants. Jefferson was keen on gardening. At Monticello he grew endless varieties of apples and grapes and flowers, so his use of gardening imagery is understandable. He ordered catalogues from Philadelphia and was a sucker for any newly imported plants. I read that Bill Clinton is trying to delay a suit against him by Paula Jones and there is some more news about Hillary's travel arrangements. Polls show Clinton is winning comfortably over poor, frozen Dole. It is difficult to imagine how Dole at his age got the nomination, or even imagined that he could appeal to these restless people who love newness because they think of their country as an enterprise. Dole comes from an era as distant as the ice age. In fact he looks as though he has been chilled and embalmed like Brezhnev as he talks about 'ethical problems in the White House'. Clinton's alleged predilection for the blowjob seems much more in tune with the times than Dole's wartime heroics as a tail-end Charlie, or whatever it was. It only reminds people how old he is. But maybe Dole believes he is throwing a line to the remains of the other America, which is moving away like an ice floe that has broken off and is drifting into warmer waters.

One of the Chinese girls asks if I would like a refill. Her name is Serena. Her little Chinese face is so smooth it looks as though it has been dipped in something, like a toffee apple.

'Everything okay? Yuh? Would you like your check now?'

I hear a trace of Hong Kong in her voice: when she says, 'would you', it comes out as 'woo yoo'. How is it that the Chinese are so adaptable when the native Indians who lived in these woods found the new realities unendurable.

I stand in the path you travel until morning; morning came quickly.

'Have a real happy Halloween,' Serena says. As I give her my money she speaks more severely: 'Pay at the desk.'

Back at the hotel there's a message from Gene Brewer, just checking to make sure I made it okay. He'll come by at six, six-thirty for a quick catch-up session. He's up at his cabin now, but I can reach him on his car phone. He's leaving right after

53

lunch. It's about a three-hour drive. His wife, his second wife, is not coming down, but he doesn't say why not.

I put the adult movie channel on and lie on my bed. I can't resist this although I feel – why? – that I should. The humping is free of any of the nuances of real life. The women are all junkies with huge silicon boobs, and the men look to me like émigré taxi drivers, with uncertain gaze and strangely barbered hair. There seems to be a formula: blowjob; missionary position; positions reversed; one man two girls; two men two girls. And then it starts again. I soon see the actor with the pained expression. There is a stab at a story line: some science fiction which involves space girls jumping into a capsule of jelly and green smoke, and being transported elsewhere in the galaxy. But this plot soon breaks down and it's back to unmotivated humping.

Now I feel sorry for these dysfunctional people who have been paid to fuck. I switch to CNN News. Clinton is making a swing through the malls of California. I fall asleep fitfully. Perhaps because of the pornography or perhaps because of Wally's remark, I dream of Thomas Jefferson. He has come in from inspecting his newly planted bean arbour, by way of the sweeping flower beds, and he pauses at the nail factory, where he has a natter with his favourite slave; he has come to his bedroom to lie down to read a book on his own-design bookstand, to find me and Gloria humping in his bed. Though not doing it in the way it actually happened – nervously, exultingly and quickly – but lewdly, in the manner of *Space Girls Come*, which I have been watching. Even in my dream I am grateful that Jefferson, so tall, turns and leaves the room.

When I wake I am very uneasy. For a start I don't remember where I am. It's becoming dark on one side, the carpark side, and it is bright on the side opening to the atrium. I am lost in one of ten million anonymous hotel rooms and I feel drained and insubstantial. I look at the digital clock, built into the bedside. It's five o'clock. I feel on my body Gloria's eager tinctures. I feel her warm and scented breasts in my hair. I feel our hearts beating, galloping. What is so unsettling is that it seems not like yesterday, but a few minutes ago at most. And maybe my guilt about abusing Jefferson's, my quondam hero's, hospitality, is guilt about my neglect of the place which, as I put it so ambiguously, nurtured me. I am unsettled, too, by the information imparted to me casually by Wally Kapinsky, that my charming exploit with Gloria is common knowledge hereabouts. I hardly knew Kapinsky, in fact I avoided him and his chums. Even back then it was clear they were bearing a grudge. I wonder what is going on here: the America so clear and rational and decent, so Jeffersonian, which I admired as a boy, particularly its invitation to pursue a life of happiness, turns out to have been a ruse, disguising what was really going on. And what was really going on, according to the Kapinskys, was a whole lotta stuff you wouldn't believe, involving gunmen, the FBI, the mob and manipulators of wealth. This Timothy McVeigh seems to be one of this breed, even in his misappropriating of Jefferson's words.

I dress shakily. The invitation specifies tuxedos; I have an old silk dinner jacket which I am very fond of, but I wonder if it would be seen as dowdy. My guess is they will all be in white or midnight blue, and the women will be wearing long dresses with corsages. The corsage is a strange custom, identical orchid sprigs contained in plastic protective bubbles, given to each girl, maybe in the spirit of equality or maybe because, following Henry Ford, there are obvious savings in standardisation.

The phone rings. Gene has arrived. I descend nervously to the lobby and there he is: Gene with an absurd, middle-aged stoutness clamped on to his once puckish self.

'Gene, how are you?'

'Dan, old buddy, you look great.'

'And you Gene.'

But the truth is, he doesn't look too good. His face is strangely slicked, as though he has just been shaving, and his hair looks unnatural, as if it has been treated in some chemical way.

'Dan. Gary couldn't come. He wanted to but at the last moment we decided it would not be a good idea. He sometimes has problems speaking, which can last for days. He's better at home. We'll go see him tomorrow if that's okay with you.'

'That's fine, whatever you say.'

'Let's go,' says Gene. 'Some of the gang are dying to meet you and they've come specially early.'

He leads me across the large lobby towards the rooms he has reserved, The Mennen Suite, which now has a large sign reading, *Welcome, Hollybush High, Class of '68*. The letters are attached magnetically to a board.

The party has already started. They are in their tuxedos and ball gowns. The gowns are strangely stiff, as though they have petrified on a hanger in a closet somewhere during a long fallow period. My first thought, which I try to choke back, is that my old schoolmates look like the people you see getting off a tourist bus outside Wesminster Abbey, wearing pale raincoats and tennis shoes, the men with cheap baseball caps on their heads, the women with squares of clear plastic. But out of this anonymity, I quickly see faces I remember, resolving themselves. Gene introduces me, guiding me by the arm, forestalling any embarrassment. The names are a sort of rough hymn — Bonnie Radway, Dinah Schmidt,

Jay Bleekman, Lisa Vanstaffen, Randy Zaintz, Fred Locke, Jim Mazaryk — a hymn whose tune I recognise gratefully, like a man going to church after a long absence.

Soon I'm swimming in warmth and conviviality. My face is covered with lipstick, generously applied for the reunion.

'Is Gloria coming, Gene?'

'There she is,' he says.

She is standing all alone, by the door. Although her breasts have welded into a bosom and although her golden-brown hair is now brindled and perhaps over-permed, making it look like a short, vigorously curled wig, she has the same soft, exceedingly sweet smile.

'Look at you,' she says, 'so suave, so elegant.'

'Gloria, Gloria, my God, the same beautiful smile.'

We kiss briefly because we must. And then she sings quite tunefully: 'The kids in Bristol are sharp as a pistol, when they do the Bristol stomp.'

And I remember the Bear's Den where we first kissed and there is an almost unbearable turbulence in my blood. Actually it is the wind created by rushing memory, like the turbulence created by a train in a tunnel.

'Gloria.'

I kiss her again affectionately, and she holds me to her frame, which is a series of ledges rather than shapes.

'Jesus, the party hasn't even started,' says Gene, 'and you're going like gangbusters.'

'You ain't seen nothing yet,' she says, with that chipper brightness that Americans now affect.

'Gloria. Seeing you was worth the fare, if nothing else.'

'You sound rather British,' she says, emphasising the 'raather', 'but I like it. How's your sister?'

'She's alive and well and doing good works. Two kids, one grown up, one marriage, now over. Still laying down the law. And you?'

'It's a long story. You wouldn't want to hear it now. Let's just say it's had its moments. But I'm fine now. Gene says you've been married.'

'Yuh. I was married for fifteen years, lived with someone else for about seven, and now I'm a bachelor again.'

'Children?'

'No. No children.'

Stephanie used to suggest that having children would be good for me. It would put me in touch with deeper realities.

'And you?' I ask.

'Nobody's told you?'

'No. Told me what?'

'There was a serial killer around about here a couple of years ago. And my daughter was one of the victims.'

'My God, Gloria, I'm so sorry.'

'He killed six women in the county, two of them students at Hollybush. My daughter was working at Hollybush in the administration office, and she was working late. He was waiting when she came out. He was caught in the end, trying to bury one of the bodies in the cemetery, in a fresh grave. The cemetery down by where we used to live. Don Conklin caught him. Do you remember Don? He's the chief of police. Anyways, my daughter's body was found over near where Peabody's Farm used to be, now a factory store. Know where I mean?'

'I drove by there today. Oh, Gloria, that's too terrible.'

I put my hands on her shoulders, and she puts hers around my waist, as though we are dancing.

'Dan, Dan, why did you run away?'

'I never ran away, Gloria, I just went with my parents back to England. And then I got caught up in being young. I just went along with it.'

Time is too short to explain to her now what it was like to be transported to the King's Road then, fresh from Hollybush. It was like being the first sea creature to crawl on to the shore and discover his gills had become lungs. The world I had left behind seemed to be composed of the wrong elements.

'You never wrote to me,' she says.

'I wrote. But I didn't send the letters.'

'Why not?'

'I can't tell you now. I really don't know. It seems awful, now that I see you, in person.'

'Less than one week after the senior trip, and you were gone.'

Around us people are gathering, waiting to speak. Gloria kisses her hand and touches it to my lips.

'Don't run away again, Dan. I want the first dance,' she says.

She moves away into the crowd as I embrace my old classmates. Jim Mazaryk comes up to me. Almost alone of all those I have met so far he looks just as he did, large, boyish, eager. His chest bows out in front of him. He seizes me by the throat with two hands and kisses me. His face is damp.

'You wrote a paper for me on Mark Twain. You remember?'

'I do.'

'Yes you did. I got an A. I forgot to thank you. That's why I'm kissing you.'

'And I used the same paper for Miss Jameson and got a B.'

'Life was never supposed to be fair. I'm glad you came back. But you'll see, believe me, nothing's turned out the way we expected back then. I guess we were living in some kind of a dream. Don't fall for the old nostalgia bullshit.'

Already I have seen that there is a theme to this: there was a better America, an innocent America which has passed.

Gene calls us together.

'Before we eat, before we hear Dan speak, before you all get too looped, can we have a photograph? Most everyone's here. Over by the bandstand please.'

There are nearly a hundred of us. We troop over to the cut-out palm trees and assemble. There is a lot of laughter, as we pretend to be schoolkids again.

'Four gone since the last ten-year reunion,' Gene tells me quietly. 'Five including Jim's wife, Shannon. She wasn't in our class. As a matter of fact she wasn't even in junior high in our day.'

The photographer tells us to shuffle closer. Gloria is standing next to me.

'Don't show the bags under my eyes,' says a voice. Someone else says, 'Don, don't moon like you did in sixty-eight.'

'Don's the chief of police now,' says Gene.

In an early version of our senior year picture, Don Conklin's bottom was facing the camera. We were all called back. We laugh uproariously; it's nervous laughter, but it's pleasurable stirring the pot of memory to see what will come to the surface. The photographs demand a moment of attention. We are aware that these reunions are in some way historic; for a few seconds we are almost reverent.

When the photographs are done and we begin to mill, Gloria moves very close to me, so that I breathe in her warmth.

'Dan, my daughter, who I named Belinda for your sister, was your daughter. She was conceived on the senior trip to Washington, most likely. She would have been twenty-seven this July past. But, Dan, I don't hold anything against you.'

This cannot possibly be true. This stout little woman with the angelic smile, the teeth so evenly spaced and white — her eyes still china blue, Lutheran, Baltic blue — this woman is deluded.

Gene calls me over to the microphone.

'Speech time,' he says. 'The prodigal has returned. And now he's going to speak to us before we sit down to the rubber chicken, because none of us can wait that long to hear from him. I give you our old buddy, Dan, Dan Silas, folks, all the way from London, England where he has become humungously rich and, as luck would have it, girls, he is looking for a real nice Michigan girl for a wife.'

4

In accordance with what principle can I say that my experiences are definitely my own?

Now, in Gene's Cadillac, heading for the town of Holland, Michigan, to renew acquaintance with our old classmate Gary Beaner, I see ever more clearly that it's a lot more than an essay topic. I want to discuss Gloria's revelations with Gene, but Gene is fully occupied filling me in on the history of our class, and I can't interrupt. The fields along the way are now loaded with snow. This is not the sort of snow which dusts or decorates the landscape. This snow has been dumped on everything, crushing the cornfields, flattening out the hills and valleys, straining the trees, entombing the houses in thick slabs. And this sheer weight, this Arctic implacability, presses on my mind too.

I asked Gene last night about Gloria's health.

'She's had her problems, you know, but hell, who hasn't? She's coming through real well.'

If it was true that Gloria was the mother of my child, Gene would have taken up my invitation to tell me what he knew, but now he is telling me about Chuck van Waning, who went off to Nam and is now a master carpenter in Spokane. When he came back from Nam, Chuck grew dope in Baja California, and became a manufacturer of surfboards, but that market kinda fizzled out and he drifted about a bit. Now he's making a good living building decks out of hardwood for second-home people, who are proliferating. Gene himself is an accountant, and he has seen, in the way that accountants do, all the craziness and folly and delusion – the whole ball of wax – which people go in for. Although the financial side is far from the whole story, you can usually read between the lines very clearly. But he feels a responsibility for our class which goes way beyond just organising the newsletter and the class reunions. Because he understands the essential simplicity of money – 'I know what makes the wheels go round' – he has initiated a small mutual fund and half the class have invested in it, 'half of those who are alive and traceable, anyhows'. It's non-profit making, except for a small management fee, and he's proud of the fact that he's helped so many people. Chuck, for example, way out in the Pacific West, was able to start his own business with the profits of just eight years.

Gene talks in a low soothing voice. In profile he doesn't have the sort of presence which would detain one's eyes for long. There's a kind of complacency in his provincial conceits. His hair has gone violently grey just at the sideboards, and his chin rests comfortably on top of a supporting roll of flesh, tightly coiled like those towels they give you on airlines, but his somewhat lifeless hair has been blow-waved so that there is a little jaunty but unnatural quiff curling towards me. He's wearing a plaid shirt and chinos. On the back seat lies his windcheater, the inside of red tartan showing. In fact he is dressed in exactly the same way as he dressed in 1968.

I was enthusiastic in my eagerness to fit in, but my mother never adapted sartorially: she liked long pale dresses and small straw hats decked with flowers, so that people used to tell me admiringly that she looked so English. Most of the time I was proud of her, but her sense of living amongst mildly amusing aboriginals made me anxious because the conformity of teenagers is rigid. Gene is on his second marriage. He tells me that his new wife, who is somewhat younger, didn't want to come down from the cabin and spoil his fun.

'You know the thing with Gayle is that, unlike my ex, she has a kind of inner peace. She has her own space, and she grants me mine. I think that's real important. Like last night, she just said, "Go Gene, you just do what you have to do. Enjoy yourself. This is your night, your class, and you've worked hard for it. I'll still be here for you, you know that."'

After I made my speech Gloria had gone, taking with her her version of what happened in Jefferson's bed. I asked if anyone had seen her, but no one seemed to know if she had left. Instead they wanted to offer me their memories of my boyhood. I spoke to them, we danced, we reminisced, we sang a school song, we had our photograph taken, Gene made a speech. All the time I was thinking about Monticello.

Protruding on an arm over the bed, Jefferson had an adjustable book holder, which I pushed to one side before – if Gloria is telling the truth – conceiving our child, who is now dead. I discovered that it is true that a serial killer operated in the area. Officer O'Keefe confirmed that last night. He was in our class, just Daryl O'Keefe then, although I couldn't remember him too clearly. He hadn't made the arrest himself, but had been called in as back up. The killer, a man from out of state called Scott Hollinger, who had become something of a loner since his wife left him, had killed six women, three of them in Hollybush or near by. Hollinger had been arrested by Don Conklin when they received a report

of a suspicious vehicle heading down Seminary Street one night. A
man walking his dog had heard faint hammering from inside the
trunk. Sheriff Conklin had followed the car and arrested Hollinger
as he was burying in a fresh grave a computer programmer from
Saginaw called Kimberley Seighardt, who was not yet dead. She'd
been revived despite being raped, almost strangled and half buried.
O'Keefe said that nothing like this had ever happened in Hollybush
before, which I could well believe, and that he personally blamed
it on the free availability of pornography: 'Don't tell me it don't
leave a mark. Sure, for ninety-nine outta a hundred, it's not going
to make any difference, but for that one it triggers something.
You remember when Mr Zabruder would put you on report for
saying "hell"? Times have changed, that's for sure.' He whistled
sadly, a sucking in of his breath over his teeth. It's true that Mr
Zabruder disapproved of the word 'hell', but O'Keefe seemed
to have forgotten that behind the Kiwanis and Rotary Club
and Redskin Boosters and church organisations, was a counter
culture, which reacted particularly intensely in a small town like
this, as though all these neat houses and bald eagle mailboxes and
basketball hoops and earnest endeavours were designed to provoke.
This has become one of the prevailing myths of America: that the
good people are really just bastards using the system. In England
we have lost any notion of absolute standards, so that judgement
is passed in ironic or coded ways. Here in mid America the urge
to pass judgement is still strong.

And now as we drive along – Gene is telling me that Jim
Mazaryk has made it to the very top of the state's Legal Department – I remember that there were one or two strange girls, Bonnie
Radway was one, who would consent to a gang bang under certain
conditions. A spokesman for a consortium of boys approached

these girls and they would, for what deep psychological reason I cannot now imagine and at the time never asked, agree to sex after a few drinks. Bonnie enjoyed the notoriety: it sat very lightly on her. And there was Bonnie last night, still quite lean, but lean in a dry middle-aged way, the pieces angulated and out of symmetry, someone whose life had fragmented cruelly: her husband was killed in Vietnam, she was divorced from her second husband, and a child had died mysteriously in Lac Blanc, Wisconsin. But among her friends she was happy, still Bonnie Radway, a girl who would do it in cars parked out by the lake. My experience of the relationship between men and women in the sexual arena is that there are compacts and understandings and trade-offs which everyone knows, but somehow were left out of the text book. And the reason for that is that sex is the plumb line into the unknowable depths, depths where we paddle haplessly, like puppies drowning.

So Officer O'Keefe has forgotten, as people who acquire authority do. And serial killing, which takes up so much of the prints and so many television hours, is the final affront to the American – and Jeffersonian – dream, because it is carried out not by crazy black people or deracinated Latinos, but by the high school misfit, the plump boy with ill-fitting glasses or by that silent boy who collected knives, or by some boy with a stiflingly Christian mother. And serial killing is in appalling bad taste, over-consumption and excess in a way Europeans – without good reason – think of as essentially American.

Gene said that Gloria had had her troubles. Had she invented the child who was murdered? I stop him for a moment as he is telling me about the excellent record of the Hollybush Redskins in the mid-state league.

'Gene, sorry, there's something I would like to ask you about Gloria. She says her daughter was one of those murdered. Is this true?'

'Dan old pal, I'm sorry to say it is true. She's had a hard time and I'm concerned that she should get over it.'

'She says the girl was my child.'

'Well, you know that was a rumour which came some time after the event. She married Fred Larssen, two years ahead of us, the assistant coach here, and she had a child very soon after. Fred and she separated after the second child, a boy, and then she apparently told Karen that you were the father and that Fred had left her because of that. But I have to tell you, Belinda looked just like Fred, same kinda big, widely spaced eyes and very fair hair. And I've seen Fred a couple of times in the last few years. He's living over near Gary, Indiana, now, and he told me that the reason they were separated was they didn't get along, just one of those temperament things. It was nothing to do with jealousy. If you ask me Dan, Gloria may have kind of tickled up the story. After Belinda was killed she went to see a psychotherapist and maybe, who knows, maybe they decided that Fred left her because of Belinda. Fred was really cut up when Belinda died. It was a horrible thing, a terrible thing, which could have deranged anybody in my opinion. I did ask Gloria not to bring the matter up with you, but I guess she couldn't stop herself, and I can't really blame her for that. Dan, you know, while you've been away a lot of water has flowed under the bridge.'

He says this with a little satisfaction, in case I have been imagining that out here in the boondocks it's all been bran-tubbing and pie-baking and lawn-mowing for twenty-five years. The truth is that I have hardly given the place a thought while the water —

a torrent apparently — was flowing under the bridge. Gene has moved on from the subject of Gloria. It is part of his responsibility to manage the news I see, as we slap through the snow-stifled farm land.

'Yep. It's all been going on in little old Hollybush, Dan. And sure, it's true some of it hasn't worked out just the way we thought it would when we signed the year books, but I'll tell you what, I don't lose too much sleep about that. That's life. People have to kind of find their own level, hack their own way through the jungle, and in that respect we've mostly turned out okay. A whole lotta people say America has changed, Dan, but I don't go along with the wimps who want to hunker down in the bunker, hoping somehow it's all going to change back. No sir. We have to go with the flow, at the same time as keeping true to ourselves, that's my belief, are you with me?'

'I am. I think I am. Gene, do you think Gloria needs help, financially anyway? I'm in a position to help her a little if you think it's a good idea. I was very fond of her.'

'Let's see now, you were so fond of her you wrote to her just the once after the high school trip. Are you being just a little sentimental, ole buddy?'

He says this without apparent malice.

'Gene, I was young, I just got caught up in a new life.'

'After Fred moved out, I paid for Belinda to go to college. She was at Lansing. But apart from that she has been able to get by. Her boy's got a job in Detroit and she works at Bronner's Christmas Store over at Frankenmuth. She's got a pretty good job there. She's a supervisor in tree trims and decorations. Sure, I can speak to her and see if she would appreciate some help. But you don't need to assume some kinda moral responsibility for her now, whatever

69

your feelings. We invited you back because we wanted to see you again. We've all taken a few lumps, but hell, as I say, that is life. And look, your life may not have been all plain sailing either, for all I know.'

'That's also true.'

Is he inviting some sort of confessional? Does he want me to tell him that my ex-wife became anorexic in her unhappiness, that she became pitifully thin and damaged her ovaries in the process? Does he want to know that Krupat and I fiddled the tax authorities by buying a holiday house through an offshore company? Of all the misjudgements I have made and the failings I have suffered, these two burn brightest in the dark hours of the night when I lie awake. I don't wish to add some appalling callousness towards Gloria to this human balance sheet. But I feel a responsibility to open myself up to the world and consequently I can't simply accept Gene's version of what happened. Gene professes to be one of those people who is open to the changes that history brings: things may have got worse, but we must make the best of them. In truth Gene probably believes that the forces of darkness are gathering, but he also believes in damage limitation. It's up to him to show some grit in an uncertain world.

For a moment, framed by the window, his profile lit by a passing car, I see a clerical portrait of him. He's become the pastor of our class, versed in all the range of human folly and fallibility. His skin, where his jaw meets the little roll of flesh sheltering under it, is shiny in the automotive light. Skin is curious stuff, very sensitive to health and temperament and happiness. The Indian girl who works in Schwindell's has skin which glistens with youthful erotic secretions — something as natural as buttermilk or the sap from the stems of figs

— nothing like Gene's shininess, which suggests a circulatory staleness.

I can't allow him to draw a line under my relationship with Gloria. I ask him about Gloria's job. He says she works at the biggest Christmas store in the world, open three hundred and sixty-three days a year.

'You remember when we were kids, Frankenmuth was just another cow town, couple of farms, a grain elevator, a sleepy drug store. D'you remember that girl, Donna-Jeanne Rattinger, no, okay well anyways, she came from Frankenmuth, a big blonde German girl, great knockers? Anyways, there was this guy Walter Bronner, and he painted signs. One day he painted a Christmas sign, Bavarian style, and someone bought it so he painted a few more, I don't know, angels and Alps and edelweiss, something like that, and that went too. Soon he sets up a little business, Walter's Christmas Store. Now it's Bronner's Christmas Wonderland and it's the biggest Christmas supermarket in the world, maybe the only one, who knows? Twelve and a half acres under one roof. You can buy anything there from a miniature Czechoslovak nativity scene carved on an acorn to a five-thousand-dollar box of tree decorations. Year round. That's where Gloria works, in the tree trims department. She wears a dirndl and a white blouse. They got an unreal turnover, something like seventy-five million a year. The whole town's gone Bavarian, although the Germans who settled there came from northern Germany originally. Remember Piet Hochmeyer? He now runs a German sausage outlet there. He's called it Fine Schwein Food. He thinks that's a real neat little *jeu de mots*. I told him it sounded Jewish and translated as hog fodder, but he just laughed. All the tourists buy his Blue Max and Red Baron bratwurst. Good business, big bucks.'

It's commonly believed that Americans have no history but they have a history as much as anyone else. What happened was that the American wilderness entranced them, newness seduced them, and history became something which had already happened on the far side of the Atlantic. History was backward looking, stifling and repressive. Its only use was as a bran tub to dip into for colourful allegories.

'Anyways, Gloria's the boss of her department and there's nothing she doesn't know about Christmas illuminations. She recommended the blue spruce with some Polish lights shaped like candles. That was her absolute number one choice. We took her advice last year, and the whole goddam thing exploded. Luckily she had told me to spray the tree with fire retardant, otherwise we would probably be living in a trailer right now. Do you remember Dillon Pendingo? He lives out this way.'

Gene's mind is floating, just the way we are in this snow storm. In England all the cars would be going two miles an hour and there'd be an air of heroic stoicism. Here the cars and trucks are barrelling into the blizzard regardless, happily insulated against what's outside. Gene is talking, talking. His eyebrows, I see, have a number of thick questing tendrils of hair which are pushing upwards and downwards strongly. They seem to be as thick as fishing line.

I try to listen to Gene, to hear what happened to Dillon Pendingo and James Griffin and Ashley Gerheardt but in the swirling snow I see Stephanie, and remember how she said to me, 'Dan, you must marry me, or I'm moving on. I have to have a new life. I know it's pathetic but I want children and all those things.' And I thought two things then, the first — so cruel — that she didn't express herself very well; and the second that she had changed her tune. Her appeal to me was that she was sexually profligate, experience gained in some rough, and never fully explained situations, and now she was telling me that what she really wanted was ... what she wanted was what Jacqueline had, the builders in, conversations about the colour of the nursery walls, a new baby-modified four-wheel drive (as if the infant might become stuck in deep mud in Notting Hill and urgently need the sort of rescue only low ratio could guarantee) and interviews with the local nursery schools ... Gene is saying that Ashley Gerheardt has a PhD and lectures six months a year on board cruise liners about personal development. As he talks, I think of Stephanie the first night we made love when she was wearing a blue dress with a very long skirt which she unbuttoned cheerily. Her hips were small and urgent and we embarked on a furious odyssey. And now I feel unease again. Maybe I have misread or failed to see any number of signs. Maybe if I had agreed to marry Steph, if I had acceded to her perfectly reasonable request, I would have been spared this unlooked-for history and the paternity of a murdered person. Or more likely, this farrago of nonsense.

The car is full of a meaty smell. It could be Gene – people do have characteristic aromas – but actually I think it's a sort of decay and its origins are obscure.

'There's our exit,' says Gene happily and we swoop off into the blizzard, grey pointillism against the countryside, which shows only as a backcloth.

'Just one thing I didn't tell ya,' says Gene, turning his soap-slicked face to me, 'Gary sometimes thinks he's an Indian. What they call a Native American these days.'

'No problem,' I say.

For the moment I'm not thinking about my old chum Gary Beaner and his delusions, I'm thinking about my own.

We can't see much in the snow, but suddenly Gene slows and points out a windmill, a huge thing flailing against the heartless, in fact utterly implacable, sky. 'Holland, Michigan,' Gene says, 'was founded in the eighteen forties by Dutch immigrants fleeing persecution.'

We visited the Netherlands a couple of times during my father's disastrous launch of the car for Benelux, and I remember a country so reasonable, so zealous in its reasonableness, that it is hard to imagine its people persecuting anybody.

'That's the only working Dutch windmill outside the Netherlands. The only one ever to have been allowed to be exported,' says Gene with satisfaction. 'It's called *De Zwaan*, The Swan.'

I don't ask why the reasonable Dutch should be so stingy with their windmills.

As we enter the town, the snow is still falling heavily, but here it is falling more calmly, in a more urban mood. We head up a street of large Victorian houses, some gabled in a distinctly Dutch style. Gene tells me that the citizens hold a tulip festival every year and that they also manufacture clogs. Gary lives with his mother who inherited her family business and mansion twenty some years ago. Occasionally Gary goes into a clinic for treatment, but there seems to be no pattern to his condition.

'There it is,' says Gene. 'Some house, ain't it just?'

We park in a driveway, mysteriously cleared of snow, and walk up a pathway to the house. It is a huge turn-of-the century place, with tall thin windows and a generous porch.

Gene winks as he pulls on the bell knob. 'Kinda quaint, isn't it?'

Deep in the house the bell sounds. It seems to ring in at least two places, suggesting that this house was once busy and noisy. It's quiet now, except for the muted noise of a distant television. Incontinent television laughter and urgent snippets of music float from a distant room. We see through the stained glass a figure coming towards us. Perhaps the glass is distorting, because the figure appears to be shuffling.

'Gary,' says Gene quietly.

The door opens slowly. The first thing I see is that my old chum has been taken apart and badly reassembled. His head is now inclined downwards, and his slender face, his delicate face, still dusted with a north-European reddishness, is seized in a painful embrace, as though it is being pulled downwards by hidden guy ropes, from which it is straining to rise.

'It's good to see you, Dan,' he says. The voice has slowed too, like a tape not running at quite the right speed. 'How are you? You look just great . . .'

I step towards Gary and take his hand. His hands are large and strong. Many Michiganders are the descendants of tall skinny Calvinists and Lutherans, grown even bigger and more awkward, with flapping hands and legs that don't always walk gracefully or in time. His hands close on mine. They are dry.

'I'm fine, Gary. I'm fine. I hear you have had your troubles but you don't look too bad yourself.'

His head is inclined downwards, but his eyes peer upwards, heartbreakingly.

Gene embraces Gary briefly.

'Dan made a real good speech last night. It's a shame you couldn't be there. Can I have a piss, I'm dying?'

'Sure. The can's through there. Go ahead. Come in Dan. Do you want some tea, English tea?'

'Yes please.'

I follow him through to a huge room, the furniture all spindly modern and slightly uneasy, too close to the floor, while the ceilings seem high and empty, far, far away, leaving an awkward vacancy above us.

'This is the day room.'

'That's great.'

There is a pause.

'Look, come to the kitchen with me, you'll be interested in that.'

I follow Gary. He is trying to speak but there is a blockage for the moment. I put an arm around him.

'No hurry. It's been twenty-seven years.'

'No hurry. I like that. No hurry.' The words pop out suddenly, and he laughs.

From inside, the laugh is pure and untouched. I feel my eyes fill with tears which I wipe hastily as he stumbles towards the kitchen. He used to be at least four inches taller than me, but because of the contortions that have taken place, we seem to be about the same size.

'The kitchen is Dutch Delft tiles. Original, from 1888. My great-grandfather imported them.'

There is a large fireplace, the back of which is all blue tiles, pictures of flowers and birds and bridges and castles. It's a strange room with plenty of Dutch knick-knacks — bellows and kettles suspended, and clogs — but also a huge old Kelvinator, the sort of thing that people in our agency liked to feature in ads, and a breakfast bar of light-blue Formica. The walls are dotted with Delft plates, picturing windmills and willow patterns.

While the kettle is boiling, Gary looks at me smiling.

'I bet you like tea. English tea.'

'I do.'

Gene appears.

'That's better. You got Dutch plumbing. It's kinda warm and cosy in here, let's sit.'

'Sure, let's sit at the breakfast bar.'

'Sit down, here.'

Gene shepherds us towards the breakfast bar.

'You remember Uncle Bob's Diner in Flint?' Gary asks me.

'I do. You and me and Gloria and Karen went there once and you put vodka in the root beer.'

'I did that?' Gary is pleased to be reminded. 'Did I really?'

'Yes you did.'

He smiles again, almost believing.

'Anyways. Bob's Diner has now been moved here just out of town. Don't you think it's crazy that something like that has become art, something we used to visit? It's because . . .'

But Gary's voice begins to thicken, and quickly chokes. He fusses with the tea. Gene helps him.

'I know what you mean,' I say.

And I do. I contributed to the iconography. I was in charge when the agency shot a commercial in Rosie's Diner in Little Fir, New Jersey. The diner, all leatherette and aluminium, was made by the Paramount Dining Car Company, just after the war, and had become a film location rather than a place.

Gary sits silently with his head apparently wedged downwards.

'He may not speak for a while. Don't worry. He's okay.'

How does Gene know he's okay? He's locked in there now, troubled. He's listening intently as though the noise inside somewhere has drowned out his speech. As Gene pours the tea he says, 'He's been looking forward to seeing you for a long time.'

We drink our tea; Gary has left us for the moment.

'Once he told me he hears music sometimes, very clearly. Not like a memory or anything like that but really playing in his head like a hi-fi.'

'You like tea, don't you Dan old sport?' Gary says, his face suddenly clearing.

'Yes I do.'

'Did you see Gloria?'

'I saw her but a little too briefly.'

'Was she looking good?'

'She was. She's got the loveliest smile. I've never forgotten it.'

'Gloria loved you, Dan.'

His face is earnest, his upturned eyes unblinking.

'It was some time ago.'

'No, she loved you. It stayed with her in her bloodstream.'

Mrs Beaner comes in to see us and Gene introduces me. She has a lean, severe dried-flower look which I remember well, like the wife in that painting 'American Gothic'. People used to talk about iceberg mothers, and she was thought to be one. Iceberg mothers could induce schizophrenia. But as a boy I always found her interesting; she liked to talk about specific topics that took her interest, and had no time for small talk. She greets me now without effusion, and asks me if I think the royal family has a future. Her face is creased, but still unsullied, like the faces of women who have been ordained, lit from within by serene candle power. She waits intently for my answer.

I tell her that in my opinion the royal family should be seen only as a symbol, the more boring the better. She considers this theory gravely: 'You may be right, the hereditary principle is hard to justify but that is why it's so darn fascinating. Democracy has contributed to the dumbing down of this country, where everybody's opinion is valuable, every damn fool's opinion is valuable, no matter how nonsensical. I must go now. Come again soon, Dan. Interesting talking with you, as always.'

She leaves the room purposefully.

'She may come back,' says Gene, winking, 'you just never know.'

'The monster mash, it's a graveyard smash,' says Gary in a sing-song.

'He hears music, like I said.'

'My mom got married again, you know, after my dad died,' says Gary, 'but her new husband Alva was interested in taking control of the business so that didn't work out. Gene helped me on that too.'

'I help a little with the family trust and so on.'

Gene pours some more tea.

'Gary, do you want to talk privately with Dan? I've got things to do, some gifts to buy. I'll leave you two for an hour or so, okay?'

'That's fine. No, that'll be okay,' says Gary.

Because his face is inclined downwards he has to look up to speak, so that his eyes are coquettish. We sit in silence as Gene leaves the house. In this kind of house his progress is easily followed: resonating footsteps, brass door fittings clashing importantly, generous sheets of glass in the inner doors protesting like ice floes, and the heavy stillness as the front door closes, like the door on a safe. The silence is broken only by the distant over-anxious scratching of the television.

I'm waiting to see what Gary has to say to me, his face long, gentle, but pulled here and there by unknown forces, as if it is preparing itself to speak.

'Come, follow me.'

As we walk through the house he begins to chant, *Man e do, we ha pe-me so win: ka wi ka da an na we was si nan.* And then he sings what appears to be a chorus: *he-he-he-he — yo.*

He takes me by the hand and leads me out of the house into the yard and across the snow in the direction of a barn.

Man e do, we ha pe-me so win: ka wi ka da an na we was si nan.

His voice is high and strained, forced through his nose and those caverns which lurk under the cheekbones.

He-he-he — yo.

Our tracks are deep, cleanly cut in the snow. He opens a small side door. The barn is cold. In the centre under the curved roof, which looks like the inside of a very large upturned dinghy, is a tent, skins stretched over a framework. There is a red post outside the entrance. I follow Gary into the tent. The floor is spread with blankets. Gary lights a lantern and sits, gesturing for me to sit opposite him. Now he chants again, *wa ka-ka, no, ho shi a de.*

I see a stuffed owl and some other animals as well as upright, carved figures that may be bears. Gary reaches for a bag made of skin and takes from it a small pouch, and from that he takes some snuff which he inhales. Then he hands the pouch to me and I do the same. The snuff scorches the inside of my nose and I cough. Tears start in my eyes. He takes a pinch of the snuff and throws it to his left and then to his right. From the bag he takes some other moth-eaten objects;

bits of animal skin, bone, and something which looks like a gourd.

Ni wi we wai a de me no a na.

He lights a long pipe and draws in the smoke before handing it to me.

Ka wi ka da an na we was si nan.

Now he takes the pipe from me, puffs, and points the stem one way, puffs again. He hands it to me and I do the same although my eyes are burning; a steady nicotine stain emerges from my nostrils as we direct the pipe to all four points of the compass.

'Try to open your heart, Dan.'

'I'll try, Gary. Just let me wipe my nose.'

He watches me with his upturned eyes as I stem the flow with a paper napkin from the hotel. The bottom half of his eyes are white, the effect of his upwardly inclined gaze.

'Are you cold?'

'Yes, I am quite cold.'

'Here.'

He drapes a large, malodorous fur cape around my shoulders.

'That is a buffalo robe. It belonged to a chief. I recovered it from the University of Michigan Museum.'

'Had it been there some time?'

'It was pillaged without regard for our people's beliefs. Your friend President Jefferson has a similar robe – a Mandan robe – at Monticello, but that one was given to him. This one was taken. This one is going back to our brothers soon. It may smell strongly but it is warm. In our language – the Ojibwa language – we say the knowledge comes from the heart. Try to open your heart to what I'm going to say. No empirical mind, no deductive reasoning, which I'm sure you used to

81

study at college in Oxford, is going to help you with this one.'

He looks at me keenly to see my reaction.

'I'm with you Gary.'

'Dan, I'm Pale Eagle, the adopted son of Wenonah and Red Deer. I was born into a family of English settlers in the Ohio Valley and captured by Shawnees and sold to my new parents near the town of Detroit, which in those days was nothing but a trading post and fort. And I grew up as an Ojibwa.'

I am sitting on the floor in a hut, wearing some mouldering skins, but I don't feel uneasy as Gary tells me his story. What do I care if he is completely insane? As he says, I am going to get nowhere by deductive reasoning. And also, it's far from certain that my own experiences are my property anyway.

5

Death is not a question in life.

I never fully understood Wittgenstein, but I have always liked this observation, which I take to mean that there are certain questions in life — and they often concern death — which cannot be answered. It is not just that you cannot find the solution, but that you cannot imagine a way to set out to answer the question. I am thinking specifically about reincarnation.

Was Gary really telling me that he is reincarnated? Is it enough to accept that he believes that he is Pale Eagle, companion at arms of the Shawnee Prophet? He still looks like a lanky, Lutheran Midwesterner, but that of course, could be no more than the surface appearance. Mad people are often sure that they are Napoleon or Jesus Christ or the handmaidens of a pharaoh, even when they look like ordinary people, ordinary people who have taken a few knocks, usually. And in some places it has become fashionable, with the aid of a trained therapist, to explore imagined past lives. But how could you begin to verify the fact of reincarnation, except as a figure of speech?

The Ojibwa, Gary told me, make no crude distinction between the quick and the dead. The dead simply inhabit a different realm, perfectly alive, but living in another place, in the upper sky as far as I can see, communing with the thunderbirds. Sometimes they have to come back to help those on earth. They might take on different forms to do this. In this case, Pale Eagle has taken on the form of Gary Beaner, of Holland, Michigan. The old Gary Beaner continues to live on as a receptacle for Pale Eagle, but in a more subdued fashion. He still lives with his mother, for instance, and takes his meals in her Delft kitchen.

We blew smoke on the manitous, the spirits, to honour them. These manitous bring power and sacred knowledge and Gary has, since his breakdown in Harvard Yard all those years ago, been acquiring this power and knowledge. When Gary told me this I saw him as a negative developing in a photographic bath. Now he is the fully finished article, Pale Eagle, a leader of his people in the final, and disastrous Battle of Detroit in 1813. He doesn't see it as the last gasp of British power in the region but as a turning point for his people, the loss of all hope as the country was opened up to the regiments of Conestoga wagons, advancing as relentlessly and almost as fast as Hitler's armoured divisions across the beet fields of Northern Europe. And the wagons brought with them a whole new set of certainties, none of which acknowledged the importance of thunderbirds or otters in the scheme of things.

And what strikes me now as I lie in the hotel watching, with hardly any interest, a man and two women fucking uncomfortably in an open convertible, is that all the beliefs and certainties of those pioneeers in the wagons have proved hardly more durable than those of the Indians they displaced. If this is true, that certainties will forever change, why should I sneer at Gary's story? As a matter of fact I don't. I am quite prepared to believe that he can read the birchbark scrolls of his people and find the sumac berry, which is a cure for diarrhoea, as well as see the future in dreams. Although I can't understand exactly how he could be a reincarnation, I have known English people who have effectively become French by living in Paris and Americans who have become indistinguishable from their neighbours in London SW3. Also I have noticed how quickly children adapt to a new town, a new country, a new accent. They do it without conscious effort. So I can believe that there is a sense in which Gary has become an Indian. I turn the television off. The ubiquitous man with the pained expression vanishes. Good riddance.

Gary has particularly wanted to talk to me, it seems, because our friendship went deeper than any other. I seem to have this ability, perhaps a handicap, for suggesting to others that I am closer to them than I feel. This has caused me some problems, particularly in the case of Stephanie. Gary believes that I should be the recipient of his special knowledge and in my present state of mind I am willing. When he told me of how he had been kidnapped as a child and brought up amongst the Indians and how he had learned to hunt, he spoke with occasional long pauses during which he would gulp as though he were swallowing an orange segment whole; his hands, those huge Baltic baseball mitts, would play with his bag of sacred objects which he said was a medicine sack. And then he stopped to chant and puff at the pipe.

We we wai a de ne noi o na.

This was a song about the medicine sack. The medicine sack contains objects of special importance, talismans. When he fasted as a boy and he was visited in his hallucinations by a bear, he made a small effigy of a bear on a piece of birchbark, and that piece of birchbark he wore around his neck until he became a man, and then he carried the effigy in the medicine bag which he showed me; the figure of the bear looking more like an ant to my untrained eyes.

The whites of his eyes were lit from below so that I thought of one of those old westerns where the Indians sit around the camp fire and a highly artificial light flickers on their faces. The Mandan robe was heavy, and I began to feel clammy. My head was light from the tobacco. There was something ludicrous about our encounter. But Gary in his slow strangled voice spoke a kind of poetry as he told me about his previous life. When he, Pale Eagle, learned to make meat, it was always done with a grave consideration for the feelings of the animals, because the animals were not just animals. We were not put on earth to have dominion over the birds of the air and the beasts of the field. This was one of the most abhorrent notions that the settlers brought with them in their wagons. Their wagons contained all sorts of contagion, fatal to the Ojibwa, Chippewa and Powatomi, but fatal to their souls as much as to their bodies.

And he showed me what was in the sack: the leg of a goshawk, some strips of skin attached to a rattle, the bear effigy, some red powder for decorating the face, which he dotted on my forehead, and some leather ties. The red dots on my face he said were to invite the manitous to shoot me with the migis, tiny pellets of knowledge. The manitous gave life as well as knowledge, in a fashion I didn't fully understand which involved the active participation of the otter.

Before I left, Gary gave me a necklace of bear claws. It is a wonderful object: the claws are three inches long, attached to a strip of flat round disks, made from shells, delicately patterned with what look like flowers.

'Do you know that these shells came from the sea, two thousand miles from here?' he asked as he attached the necklace to my throat which entailed some wrestling with the bulky buffalo robe. And I could see that he was suggesting that a wealth of meaning was contained in that question: how the shells had travelled down the Indian highways and been bartered, how they had been chipped and shaped into these perfect disks and threaded and etched, and I guessed that to Gary the shells spoke of free movement on this great continent, this world which Ronald Reagan once said lay there waiting to be discovered by the pioneers.

'We believe that if you wear this necklace, you will be invisible to your enemies.'

There are many stories about charms which make you invisible. You can also take potions or rub on ointments. Perhaps I could try out the necklace by visiting Stephanie. I have a considerable interest in her present sexual arrangements. (Hints of new beginnings have been dropped.)

When Gary and I walked back to the house, Gene was sitting patiently in the Delft kitchen reading *Popular Mechanics*. We had been in the foetid tent inside the barn for three hours. Gary was silent. Gene said nothing about the dots on my face which looked in the mirror like livid chicken pox spreading in a band across my forehead – where there is sadly plenty of space – and dotted on my cheekbones. The decoration on my face was like shot marks on a pheasant's rump.

In the car Gene said: 'Did he take you inside his lodge?'

'The lodge. That's what you call it?'

'Did you go inside?'

'Yes.'

'I've never been inside.'

The blizzard had died. All traces of grey had gone; the sky was like squid's ink.

'How crazy is he, Gene?'

'Sometimes I am not sure if he is crazy at all. He has to go in for drug therapy when he gets too wound up, but you know when you're talking to him, you soon forget that his whole world is based on some real crazy premises. It all makes some sort of sense.'

And I thought that maybe Gene was talking of Gary's personal poetry which was simply another way of grappling with the unknowable.

We were silent then, as people often are on return journeys. But I was thinking that the white man's beliefs are no more rational than the red man's. Nor do they provide a remedy against death. And now people are growing suspicious of science; they think that doctors are hiding the truth; that nuclear physicists are conspiring to destroy the environment; that police laboratories are fakes; that armies experiment on their troops with drugs. And they say all these things because they have finally realised what should have been obvious all along, that science does not extend beyond the grave. They feel cheated. They have been deceived, and somebody is going to pay.

Death is not a question in life.

As we floated along the highway in the inky night, I saw Pale Eagle making his childhood journey through the deep snow and across the freezing rivers, ever deeper into the forest, ever further from the nervous clusters of farms and cabins and sawmills on the

Ohio. And I imagined it, as one does the illusions of great art and literature, in the most real fashion possible. As he described it, the noise of the runners of the sled on the snow and the dip of the paddles into the water became a sort of lullaby. A lullaby with its simple, repetitive rhythms enters a child's being. It stays there, somewhere in the most minute components of the body, until death.

Gary said his memories of his early life were aroused in this way: he was canoeing as part of a therapeutic exercise of the Pontiac State Mental Facility to which he had been transferred from a similar place in Boston after his breakdown, and when the party had been canoeing on Lake Superior for a few days he began to remember the rhythm and the exact sound of the paddles. His previous life came back to him, not suddenly, but in snatches the way you can remember a few words of a song, and then a whole chorus and, most evocative of all, the way a forgotten scent of childhood – of bread dough or damp earth or a flowering plant – can summon lost emotions. Gary had the growing feeling that he was not the person whose name appeared above his bed. From that moment his true identity began to assemble itself. He was able to remember the names of trees and plants in the Ojibwa language; it started with the black spruce and the jack pine but soon became quite comprehensive, a whole arboretum. And then he remembered chants and these chants were not just songs but had some greater significance. They turned out to be the songs of the Mide. I wondered if the Pontiac hospital perhaps used drugs indiscriminately as mental hospitals are prone to. And he told me that one day he ate a bracket fungus which he found in the hospital grounds growing on an oak, and he knew that the fungus was both edible and emetic, and then he began to realise that he had an extensive knowledge of natural pharmacopoeia, and he treated himself and threw away the pills the shrinks were providing. He started to treat other patients. The grounds were extensive and he gathered berries and roots. It was only a few months, less than a year, before he was able to go home, now with the aim of fully recovering his old life. He attributed his breakdown at Harvard to a crisis of competing identities. His knowledge of the Mide (which white people crassly called the Grand Medicine society) had set up some protesting 'vibes' — he winked at me as though he knew I was the sort of guy who would use such a word a lot. He told me about his friendship with Tecumseh and how he had been at his side during the hopeless Battle of the Thames, and how Tecumseh had been killed and his body never found. It was a great loss to his people, one that could never be repaired while his resting place was unknown. *It has left a gap in our hearts, through which the wind is still whistling.* Tecumseh said that the Great Spirit had made the land for the use of all his people. It could never be sold. Nobody could hold title to land.

I wondered why Gary was able to talk there in his lodge so freely, whereas back in the Dutch kitchen, *de keuken*, he had struggled with the mechanics of speech as he wished us goodbye, his large mouth several times opening and closing before a few words came out.

Gary's face as he told me his story had taken on the obdurate, stunned, wistful look you see in early photographs of Indians, as if they have just realised the way things are going. The buffalo cloak was itchy. Gary was speaking with a slight slur now, as though he were tired, but his voice was measured. He asked me suddenly if I owned a dog. I told him that I did. He wanted to know what colour it was and I described, as best I could, the colouring of a wirehaired dachshund. (There are three basic colours.)

'We have no dog totem,' he said.

'No dachshund clan?'

'Can we speak some more tomorrow?' he asked.

'Of course. I have a hire car and I'll come out and see you now I know the way.'

'Dan, we have miles to go'.

'Robert Frost.'

'You haven't forgotten.'

We had loved Robert Frost.

As we drove back to the hotel, I think Gene was resentful that I had, after all these years, simply walked in and been admitted to the lodge, talking intimately for hours with Gary while he waited in the kitchen with *Popular Mechanics*. Or maybe Gene was in on the whole thing in some way I hadn't yet seen. Stephanie told me many times that I missed the point. She had come round to the opinion that men very often missed the point. I had been troubled by this possibility. Actually the belief that men are idiots is widespread. Many of the commercials we made reflected this. When the Japanese looked at our show-reel they exchanged minute glances, and I saw that they were confirming by this delicate semaphore their conviction that Westerners are weak-minded and decadent.

'What goes on in there, Dan, in the lodge?'

'He has some Indian things. Quite a collection.'

'I've never been in the barn even, though I know he keeps souvenirs in there. Looking at you, I'm not sure as I would want to. One thing, for which I must praise the Lord, is that he has never put spots on me. You look sick,' he said jovially.

I could only see his face in the occasional snapshot light of passing cars, but in these brief flashes I didn't see any signs of resentment. Instead I saw a man who had given his spiel, made his pitch, expended his conviviality and was now drained, turned in on himself. Maybe it's true, I thought, that Americans are trying to sell themselves, to present themselves, believing that the individual is the unit of exchange. What a burden. At Hollybush we used to vote for most popular boy and most popular girl, and there were some who worked for it and failed and became bitter. Back in England I found that the fashion was to shun any obvious form of personal promotion and I quickly and all too predictably adopted the fashion.

When we pulled into the hotel sliproad, Gene stopped the car and reached for a box of Kleenex.

I wiped my face.

'Maybe you should take the voodoo necklace off too. They may think you're a weirdo.'

'It's the dachshund totem.'

'Biggest fucking dachshund I've ever seen.'

'Can we talk seriously about Gloria before I go home, Gene?'

'Sure ole buddy, that's fine. Call me tomorrow. It's been a long day and Gayle is fifteen years younger than me. You know what that means. Call me in the office tomorrow.'

He winked as he drove off in the Cadillac into the American vastness.

✻   ✻   ✻

92

Once this amplitude was familiar to me; now it is disturbingly foreign. My former best friend is singing to the spirits out there somewhere, and here in the hotel porn movies are playing in every room and the local Kiwanis have finished their chicken and are farewell-scrimmaging in the lobby and two immensely fat people are heading for the hot tub holding hands and the busboys are speaking Spanish. And somewhere out there in the biggest Christmas store in the world, is a woman who claims to have borne my child, a child who was murdered.

I remove the bear necklace from my pocket and put it around my neck. I glance at myself in the mirror. I am not invisible.

Not to myself, anyway.

6

A strange thing happens to me in hotels: I think expansive thoughts. It's being alone, of course, but it's not just that; I have been alone a lot recently. Perhaps it's being estranged from your possessions and the small things you have put in place to confirm – to yourself – your existence: books, photographs, a few paintings, a rug or two, some plants, a few old letters. On the walls there are reprints of Audubon's bird paintings; there are glasses which are sealed with a frilly hat of paper; there's a stiff shower curtain and a band of paper around the lavatory. The chairs are covered in a pale green, intensely stain-resistant fabric. The air-conditioning unit under the window has strange fibres in its works. The bed is wide and rectangular. Along the hall is a huge, unapologetic, Coke machine. I can hear from my room the thunk of cans falling and tumbling at all times of the day and night. And I feel impelled towards thought, as though just to sit here eating a club sandwich or watching the television would be to accept this as my natural habitat. In one of the prints a giant loon is drying its wings, standing on a rock, which I imagine is its natural habitat.

Stephanie believed that I was prone to think these kinds of thoughts as an escape from responsibility. She was never impressed by my argument that ultimately we have no responsibility, even though I never added, 'except to ourselves'.

I think about what Gary (I am almost ready to call him Pale Eagle in my own mind) told me: that as a boy in his previous, more outdoorsy life, he was encouraged by his adoptive parents Red Deer and Wenonah to fast. Fasting produced intense dreams and the capacity to dream was highly prized. As a small boy he had once fasted for eight whole days. And the dreams produced by fasting had set him on the road to being a shaman. He doesn't use that word, but that is what he is. And I think about the shadow world, and how easily it appears for the Indian people to pass between the two worlds, and I feel a sense of guilt that I have not really ever thought of what my father might be up to in the shadow world since his death last year. I have always assumed that death is the end, full stop, *nada*, except insofar as a deceased's essence lingers on in the memory and affections, or less intimately, is responsible for works of art. But now I wonder if this is true. In the intensified state of mind induced by being alone in this hotel, surrounded by a carpark where blocks of snow lie grey and solid, like cement bags left in the rain, and where the air itself seems to have been emptied by winter, where I am myself in the shadow world, completely disembodied, at least here I wonder about the distinction between the quick and the dead. My father's death: he was carrying a tray when he fell over with a heart attack, flinging the tea, painstakingly laid out — milk jug, hot water, strainer, teapot with insulating woolly coat — against the wall, judging by the stains that were there when I arrived some hours after the body had been removed. I never saw him dead. I could have asked to go to the funeral home for a last view, to have the coffin unscrewed. Instead I responded to the impulse to tidy everything away fast, as if his death were indecent, as if he were an old man wandering around with his trousers undone, rather than simply dead.

Trying to be sympathetic, Stephanie said, 'When your parents die you realise you are next in line for the drop.' It is true that the process of heart-hardening had been going on for a while, and I was inclined to put the worst interpretation on anything she said, but this made me angry. It was banal, said for effect only. It wasn't the fact that I had shuffled foward in the mortal line which troubled me, but that so much had gone unsaid between my father and me that might have been said. Unimaginable things, that would have elevated our relationship and given it some lustre. He had struggled to speak to me intimately, and I had never given him the means, as I might have.

And I see now that although my old chum Gary Pale Eagle may be completely nuts, what he has done is strangely sane: he has worked out an explanation for his life's circumstances which satisfies him. In that respect he has been more successful than many. Anyway, is it more absurd to believe that he was once an Indian foundling than it is to believe that we are here for a divine purpose? We are concerned here only with types of irrationality.

These kinds of thought, strangely uplifting, assail me. Hotels never advertise their thought-inducing qualities. Instead they promise conviviality and show pictures of people dining and quipping and conversing with pert members of staff. They never show men thinking ontological thoughts as they watch porn movies, lying on unmade beds beside the woodpile of cocktail sticks and the mounds of ketchup-soiled lettuce that junk food leaves behind. And, I have observed, hotel publicity never features lone women, because women on their own are thought to be in an unnatural state. A woman eating alone in a restaurant is an affront. A woman whose husand has left her is culpable in some way.

In the hotel mish-mash — the profligately used towels scattered on the floor, the violently scented shampoo bottles and soaps all opened, the Jackson-Pollocked plates, the brown Formica tray awash, the spreadeagled *Flint Journal*, the vacuum flask of luke-warm, thin coffee, the tangled and bristling sheets, and from outside the muffled rumble of human congress, a shunting yard of human folly, penetrated by the higher registers of laughter and the clash of plates as the busboys collide, I imagine — in this happy confusion I am reclining thoughtfully, when the phone rings. I start. Even the sound of an American phone is strange to me.

'Hello.'

'Hi. Dan, is that you?'

'Gloria. Gloria, Gloria, Gloria. Where did you get to?'

'I had to go. The Christmas season, in case you hadn't noticed, is almost here. We're rushed off of our feet. Did you go see Gary?'

'Yes. What time is it?'

'Just after one.'

'In the night?'

'Yes, in the night. I just got back from work. How was Gary?'

'He's become an Indian. That was interesting. Do you see him sometimes?'

'Not too often. He doesn't speak a lot and that makes me just a tad uneasy.'

'He spoke to me.'

'What did he say?'

'All sorts of things. Can I see you soon?'

'You can see me now. I'm downstairs.'

'Give me five minutes to clear up.'

What does she want at this time of night? I pile the detritus on to the tray and put it outside before straightening the sheets. A fire truck or an ambulance whoops somewhere beyond the window, adding cruelly to my unease. What does she want? Has she come to berate me? Or maybe she has the idea that we can pick up where we left off in Jefferson's long but thin bed. I am wearing a t-shirt with some underpants. Quickly I pull on the complimentary robe from the bathroom, ready to greet Gloria with the words *Holiday Inn Garden Court* on my breast.

Soon there is a knock on the door. Gloria is standing there in the durably carpeted, unnaturally wide hallway, wearing a light raincoat. There is a certain challenge in her blue eyes, but her smile is as sweet and girlish as it was back in Henry Ford's museum. She kisses me lightly.

'Surprised to see me?'

'A little. Very surprised, to tell the truth. But pleased.'

She takes off her coat. Underneath she is wearing Bavarian costume: green pleated skirt, white blouse with a scalloped neck, an apron and black shiny, solid shoes.

'Dah-dee-dah dee, da da dah,' she says.

'I didn't know you were Bavarian.'

'There's a lot you don't know, Danny.'

'That's true. Something to drink?'

'I'm in my work clothes. This is what we wear.'

'Nice. Gemütlich.'

From my minibar I am able to assemble some nuts and a club soda for Gloria, and the kettle is soon agitating and sighing. She sits on the green armchair and I settle on the edge of the bed. She may be middle aged in an absurd Alpine costume, but her eyes haven't changed. The blue is now slightly dusty. I have the feeling that we could make love, forgetting everything except our youthful eyes. The kettle boils, sending out urgent clouds of steam.

'Do you remember Henry Ford's steam-train?' she asks as I jump up.

'Puffing Billy?'

'No, it was called the Village Railroad.'

'That's right. And do you remember the Cotswold Forge?'

'Would that be the old stone house where you put your fingers in my panties?'

'That's the one. I was thinking about that and the senior trip, and what you said about Monticello.'

I pour myself some coffee. The plastic paddle for stirring the white slurry slips from my fingers and I knock the cup over.

'Are you nervous, Dan? You nervous to see me?'

'No, it's just that I was lying half awake. I only got back from Holland about eleven. I'm dazed and confused.'

'Sleepless in Seattle.'

'Or somewhere.'

I settle down again, with a scalding Styrofoam cup in my hand. The coffee, or perhaps the creamer, has a mineral taste which I try to locate in the lexicon of forgotten sensations.

'Could you tell me more about Monticello, you know, about what you said at the reunion,' I say.

'The connectedness of events. You were quite good, playing up to the hicks. Monticello, let me see now, would that be the Jefferson historic home in Richmond County, Virginia?'

'It would.'

'Let me tell you one thing, Dan, I wasn't a virgin when we did it in his bed.'

'Good God.'

'Jealous?'

'No, no it's not that. God no. It's more that I have lived all these years thinking somehow that was the moment. How do I put this without causing offence? — that was a big moment for you. Just as it was for me. We seemed to have spent most of the year working up to it.'

'You worked up to it by screwing Bonnie Radway and Jo-Anne Kelly, am I right?'

'You may be. You probably are. I don't remember. But what I meant was, our particular little odyssey to Jefferson's bed. I thought there was a kind of progress, almost something sacred.'

'Dan, let's face it, you were always good at believing what you wanted to. You thought you were on a mission. By the way, "our little odyssey", is a funny way to describe it.'

'I'm sorry. Look, I have had all sorts of surprises on this trip. As Gene said, a lot of water has flowed under the bridge. Who was the lucky boy who preceded me?'

'How do you know it was just one?'

'I don't. Let me re-phrase my question, who were the marching band who preceded me?'

'Does it matter to you?'

'It matters because of what you said the other night.'

'She was yours, Dan. I promise.'

'Gloria, why did you never tell me?'

'Don't you remember Dan, you vanished? You wrote a couple

of times, and then silence. Nothing. I came to London to look for you, when I knew.'

This can't be true. However, her eyes, strangely lit from within, like Japanese lanterns, seem to be beaming a higher truth to me. (I think of those ships which used to send each other messages by means of Aldis lamps; I feel profoundly saddened.)

'Did you find me?'

'I watched you for a couple of days. You were living on Fulham Road.'

She pronounces it 'Full-ham', but the truth of it hurts; it is piercing.

'Gloria, Jesus, why didn't you speak to me?'

'You looked like you had . . . you looked like you had another girl. I went back home two days later.'

I feel something in me lurch. It's like a ship bumping into an unknown mass in the night.

'Gloria.'

'I married Fred. Fred accepted Belinda as his own. I think Fred loved her more even than our own child.'

'I can't believe you didn't tell me.'

'How could I? I saw you there, with this girl, with two girls actually, and you walked right by me. I was only seventeen, from the sticks. I was struck dumb.'

Tears are pressing against the back of my eyes. I see the girl – now a solid woman in a green skirt, trimmed with a border of edelweiss – I see her now young and pregnant, heavy breasted, watching me, no doubt in my velvet suit and purple shirt, parading myself in the full fatuousness of youth.

'Oh Gloria, I am so sorry.'

'On the second night I saw you again. You went into

a place called Alexander's on King's Road. It was underground.'

'Alexander's, my God. I haven't thought about it for years.
It's closed.'

For a moment I am distracted, lost down there with my new
velveteen friends.

'I could never forget the name. It was the last time I
saw you.'

I stand up from the bed and try to take her in my arms. She
doesn't resist but there is no warmth or urgency. I kiss her cheek
— it is still cool from the outside air — and I sit down again on
the bed. She sits too, her eyes clear but, I think, staring somewhat
sightlessly.

'Are you working long hours?' I ask.

'We're all working long hours. But we get well paid this time
of year.'

'Gene says you are the world expert on Christmas lights.'

'I do trims as well. But yes, basically I am known as the
Christmas-tree gal.'

'I was talking to Gene and I asked him if you needed anything,
just really as a general question, and he said you were doing fine
under the circumstances, but I could ask anyway.'

'So?'

'So now I am asking. Can I help you in any way?'

'It's too late. Our girl is gone. I'll never get over it, never
ever, but I have learned something. There I was for, heck, nearly
ten years at Bronner's, first I was in crèches — you know what
they are?'

She says the word again, the upward inflection, 'crayshes'; I
think she is talking about shellfish for a moment.

'Crèches? Where the mother and the Baby Jesus are in the stable and the animals and Joseph look on?'

'Crèches. Nativity scenes. Oh yes, I get it.'

'I was in charge of crèches for a good long while, and it never occurred to me that crèches are a spiritual thing. That's how dumb I was. I thought they were cute, naturally, but I never realised that they come from a long tradition. Saint Francis had one featuring a live ox in Greccia in twelve twenty-three. Twelve twenty-three, think of that. I did some research.'

'You were always good at history.'

'But it's like I never saw history as having any connection with life. Anyways, it was only when Belinda died that I saw that we all have a kind of spirituality within us. An inner child. That's when I saw the crèche scenes with new eyes. They're called *presepioni* in Italy, by the way, where they originated from. I just slipped that in seeing as how you congratulated me on my history. I saw centuries of craving for inner peace in those little figures. And I was sorta freed up from some of my worst thoughts. I feel now that I am in touch with Belinda, even though I miss her physical presence. So I guess what I am saying is, I have most all of what I need right now.'

'I'm sure you do. I am very pleased. I just wondered if you wanted some help with, I don't know, a holiday or your apartment or whatever?'

'I don't need money, Dan. But I appreciate your offer. I really do.'

She smiles that sweet, wistful smile, but now I imagine that she pities me; she sees a person who has not achieved inner tranquillity, nor encountered the inner child. She sees a person caught in the ego traps which the world sets for the unwary.

And it's true that I have been caught up, although I have also been aware of the transience of what I was doing. But it was also pleasurable to think these thoughts. A certain self-congratulatory detachment told me that I, at least, could see the wood for the trees. I chafed some warmth into my soul by telling myself that our business required an understanding of the fleeting. I even claimed that we had made a contribution to the changed national mood, which Krupat called 'presentism'. The British, he said, were fed up of living in the past. Contrary to the received wisdom, they didn't give a stuff about history; they wanted to live in the present, embrace the present, fuck it senseless. (That was some time before the Japanese entered our lives, when he adopted more measured language.)

What I am offering in my awkward fashion to the Christmas-tree gal, whose bodice laces are loosening, is Japanese money. The Japanese are aware that their culture prevents them from embracing the present fully, so they bought us. To them it was like buying the service of a golf professional or a sushi chef, a useful but essentially mechanical skill.

'How long ago was the ... when did Belinda die?'

I cannot say the word, not because I am overcome by emotion, or the horror of the event, but because I feel a certain fastidiousness. I don't want to be drawn into this.

'Dan, you can say it. The killing. You can say it. I am past that stage. For a while there I couldn't say it either. It was two years ago last Thanksgiving.'

'Oh, okay.'

'It took me a good long time to express my grief, but once I started down that path, it became easier. But there's one thing which still sometimes wakes me in the middle of the night. Do you know what it's like to sit upright suddenly and your eyes are wide open and your skin is damp?'

She asks me this without expecting any comparable depths of understanding from me. The stays on her Bavarian bodice are now untied, giving respite to her bosom, which had been forced, in the Alpine tradition, upwards. The bodice is also trimmed, I see, with a little border of flowers. Her eyes have become bright and urgent. They seem to take on light, like the surface of a pond.

'Your eyes are so beautiful,' I say.

'You said that to me at Monticello.'

'Did we have time to speak? I don't remember.'

'We spoke a little.'

'To answer your question, yes, I do know what it's like to wake up in total confusion and despair. It's truly horrible. I don't want you to think that my whole life has been plain sailing, just a day out. Nobody's is.'

But I don't go on. This is her confessional, not mine. I could tell her how carefully I have contrived to avoid difficulties and evade irksome responsibilities. I could tell her that childlessness has reproached me with the thought that I have somehow missed the full human experience. And I could tell her that I can't now accept the parentage of a dead child I never knew.

'Are you okay?' she asks.

'I'm fine, go on.'

'I try to put off going to bed. I even work late, like tonight. I'm little Miss Available if they got problems with the roster. It's because at his trial when he pleaded guilty, no real details were given in court of how the victims died. I want to know if she suffered.'

'Gloria, of course she suffered.'

'I know. But I have to hear if he killed her slowly or quickly or whatever. She was not too badly lacerated, just strangled with her pantyhose apparently. He would bite some of the women. But no details were given of Belinda. Can you help me find out?'

'I am not sure how I would do that, Gloria. Can I think about it? See if I can find anything out?'

'Sure, of course, it's a big decision. Major. Dan, can I stay* with you tonight?'

'Of course.'

'We never spent a whole night together, you know that?'

I appear to be headed for the shadow world. I am being drawn there, wherever it is.

'What's his name?'

'Who?'

'The killer?'

Even to say the word seems to invite complicity in this madness.

'Scott Hollinger.'

The tops of her breasts are veinous, like a pregnant woman's.

After the killing, Gloria was so desperate that she would travel to Kansas City by bus and stay in a cheap hotel in order to attend a victims' support group, which met on the first Friday of every month. She would meet with these other relatives of the murdered. Now there is a nationwide organisation based in Cincinnati, sponsored by the Catholic Church; it rents a basement in Our Lady of Sorrows Church, and she goes there whenever she can. She keeps in touch with other families. You would be surprised how many there are, black, white, Asian, you name it. The danger is to avoid obsessive-compulsive disorders, she says, to which victims' relatives become liable. (I wonder, of course.)

'Did Fred ever come with you?'

'No, Fred always knew Belinda was your daughter. He was in denial for a long time, but he knew. He kinda cleared off for good when she was killed.'

'Gene says that Fred never expressed to him that Belinda might not be his daughter.'

I seem to be picking up the circumlocutions fast.

'He wanted to believe she was his daughter, sure, but he knew the truth. And besides, Gene doesn't know everything, although he likes to think he does.'

'And when you said to me you weren't a virgin when we had our, what do you want to call it, encounter, at Monticello, what did you mean?'

'I was telling the literal truth. When I was fifteen a couple of seniors got me drunk and had sex with me. I don't think I was complaining too much, but I was out of it.'

'That doesn't count.'

'When I was going with you, I was trying to forget it. I had repressed the memory, I guess.'

I make some more coffee; there is only half a sachet of creamer left, which I divide. Gloria has some honeyed pecan nuts, smokehouse flavour.

'Can I get right in?' she asks.

'Please, be my guest.'

I am playing host here. I am very ill at ease, not sure what is expected of me. I lie on the bed next to her, her body a mound under the covers. I put one arm around her, feeling a chunky solidity, accentuated by the heavy cover. I have mostly been in the company of women who were naturally or unnaturally thin, but I feel a powerful urge to embrace Gloria, in her Bavarian outfit, and somehow make up to her for what she has been through. I kiss her on the mouth.

'No Dan, let's just sleep here together. This is not the time.'

I let some leaden moments pass.

'Gloria, why did you come here tonight, really? Just to talk?'

'I came because I want you to help me, if you can.'

'I want to help you. You know that. What can I do?'

'You can visit the killer in the State Penitentiary and talk to him, Dan. He sent me a message via his lawyer, but I can't go. I just can't. He has something he wants to tell me, in person. Some last words.'

'What would be the good of that? What could come of that?'

'You could talk to him as her father, and see what he has to say. I have to know. It's tormented me.'

7

'This is the Chippewa bannock. That's what the white people call it. Except most white people take no notice of Indian customs. We make it with corn-meal, water and hazelnut oil. Here, put some maple syrup on it.'

The Chippewa bannock cake is delicious. Gary is standing by the old Westinghouse range, which has large dials and timers, watching me, ready to fry up another cake if I want one. The Westinghouse reminds me of the cars my father used to promote.

'More? Another one?'

'No more, that was fine. Enough already.'

Gary's voice today comes in spurts, like a faucet with airlocks in the pipework behind. I want to ask him about Gloria, but he has other things on his mind. I've called the State Penitentiary and discovered that it is alarmingly easy to gain access to the murderer. I was hoping that proof of paternity would be required but it seems that Gloria's nomination of me for the Perpetrators' Access Program is sufficient. She told them some time ago that I was coming all the way from England, and the path has been smoothed.

There is a sudden rush of words from Gary, who is standing awkwardly with the pancake pan in one hand and a spatula in the other.

'Dan, I want to make you wild rice with green onions and eggs before you go home. That's wild rice which our people harvest on the shores of Lake Superior, green onions, also wild, and eggs from wild birds, but you can use supermarket eggs if you want to. This is really something else, this stuff. You know, in the spring and the fall I go out into the woods and I have learned the places where the plants grow that we use. It's part of my training.'

He watches me eat.

'All done? Let's go out to the back now.'

Gary has told me that there are some things he wants to show me, and a favour that he would like to ask of me. We walk through the snow, now pockmarked and honeycombed, towards his barn. For the moment it is like an empty theatre, with dust in the air and strange dead scents. He gives me my buffalo cloak to wear and he puts on an enormous necklace of what looks like quills and bone, so that it forms a kind of chain-mail around his throat and down over his chest. He asks me to put on my bear-claw necklace. He is holding a stick which has feathers attached. We sit on a mat, and he lays the stick down and lights some tobacco from a pouch and fills a pipe. I draw in, not too deeply. (Rush Limbaugh has been making crude jokes about Bill Clinton's inhalation.) I wonder if the tobacco is perhaps hallucinogenic. My eyes sting.

We smoke to the east, south, west and north. Gary reaches for a drum and beats it briefly and harshly. He chants:

Wa ka-ka no, ho shi-a de.

'I am calling the makwa manitou, the bear spirit,' he explains. 'It takes some time.'

I'm not impatient. I'm sure you can't rush these things. I see as if from a little distance two old school chums, one crazy, one questing in a low-level sort of way, sitting on Indian rugs in a shelter, me slightly clammy in my Mandan robe (the temperature outside has risen above freezing) and Gary chanting Ojibwa, and my mind is happily free; it floats. I think of a boat and a gentle current, and of my days puttering around Squaw Lake. Perhaps Gary failed to tell me all the ingredients of the Chippewa bannock. 'Bannock', I am sure, is a Scottish word, and I see now missionaries trying to make sense of the Indians and trying to make familiar the utterly strange. Of course it is virtually impossible to think yourself back into the world of the first missionaries and explorers. All too easy now to see how they misapprehended everything then, unaware that all religious custom and rituals serve the same purpose in all human societies, namely to explain death. That is what I believe.

Gloria left early in the morning. She had to go to the Christmas supermarket because of the seasonal pressure. Sales of Christmas tree trims were at their height, although she thought I would be surprised how many people would buy them year round. Mostly older people, who arrive by the busload from all over, including Ontario. She left the number of the Correction Services' PR man, who was expecting my call.

Gary stops his chanting and looks at me, his eyes turned upwards from his locked position. He tells me about Tecumseh and his brother Tenkswatama, who predicted an eclipse of the moon. This event gave him enormous credibility. In his lodge Gary's speech has lost its halting, staccato quality and becomes dark and flowing. His hair, once red, is the colour of an Irish retriever's. His face assumes the serious impassive Indian mien, but still I see traces of the Lutheran and North European in the thin features, features of so many of the shopkeepers and teachers I knew in my youth. Not only are Gary's features unmistakably from the old pattern book, but they also contain that elusive Americanness that I now recognise so clearly. It is as though the mixture of the genes, Swedes, Germans, Dutch and so on, have produced a type resident in all the quiet white backwaters of America. As well as goofy-looking people with large appendages, this mixing produces healthy, innocent-looking people who go on to be models in Milan or golf professionals; but somehow they're not important any more. Their genes have been diverted into a backwater as the American maelstrom rushes on. They're as awkward and irrelevant as the huge and elaborate furniture that takes up so much space in their houses.

'I have prepared for you a small bag of hunter's medicine.'

'What's in it, Gary?'

'It's a secret which we learn as initiates. But I can tell you that it contains plants' leaves and roots ground into powder. When my people hunt they drop some into the barrel of their gun. We also have medicines for poison, made from the rattlesnake, the bitter black cherry and the ghost moccasin, the giant puffball. You won't need that.'

He gives me a small sack, like the tobacco pouch my grandfather used, made of soft leather, probably buckskin.

'After the Battle of Detroit, Tecumseh's body was never found. The warriors returned to their villages to know their fate, and they hoped that Tecumseh's bones would be returned for burial as is our custom, but no word was ever received of where they were concealed. We thought that the Americans may have destroyed them, because they were frightened of Tecumseh, who had the gift of oratory. Maybe they thought that if his bones were properly buried, his people would take up his work again and unite. It's too late now for our people ever to claim everything that was theirs, but my life, my new life, has been devoted to restoring to our people their beliefs and their integrity. I need your help, Dan. There are some things I want to recover for my people.'

'What things?'

'They're in your British Museum.'

'What are they?'

'They're sacred scrolls, migration scrolls in the words of songs, many of them forgotten, mnemonics. We must have them back. They are our Magna Carta.'

'Have you asked?'

'We have tried. But it's no use. The museums fob us off. They tell us to prove our claims to them and the only claims they recognise are documents, but of course all the documents of that period were written by them. They don't accept the oral history or the birchbark record.'

'How do you expect me to get them?'

'You would have to take them.'

'I can't do that.'

'Dan, there are the remains of 20,000 of our people in the Natural History Museum alone.'

I ponder this. What does it mean?

'You must wear your necklace and use the medicine I've given you.'

'I've got to take the medicine?'

I'm thinking of the giant puffball and rattlesnake ingredients and wondering how scrupulous a pharmacist Gary is.

'No, you don't need to take it, no, no. You just use it in the traditional way. I will show you how.'

Gary Pale Eagle begins to hear his internal music again. He seems to forget me. He chants: *Ha na wa na ha wa, ha na wa na ha wa.*

His voice is strangled. It reminds me of my own attempts to speak French, particularly the vowels, when I adopt an entirely alien intonation, and even essay some Gallic head and hand movements. The chanting is interspersed with the tobacco ritual, but I cannot do more than pretend to smoke from the pipe. The air inside the lodge is now heavy. As well as the tobacco spiralling pungently in the gloom, there are the scents of skins and rugs and baskets and the otter medicine bags and the war sacks, and the eagle feathers attached to streamers of bison and deerskin, the artefacts of bone and porcupine and antler and shells. In here, I see, Pale Eagle enters his Indian world while just across the yard his elderly mother is thinking her own, deeply Lutheran thoughts.

Gary's chanting becomes conversational. Perhaps the bear spirit is talking to him. I would be pleased if it were. My eyes are heavy.

I was up late. Gloria had suggested to me that I had forced her to have sex in Jefferson's bed. Just after she said this she fell into a heavy sleep, leaving me in a state of shocked wakefulness. And now, with Gary's request that I steal things from the British Museum, and Gloria's disturbing claims, I'm beginning to wonder if Gene, the carbolic-cheeked Gene, is not in on this whole business. According to Gloria, I said if she didn't do it with me then and there I would ring the firebell. This detail seems absurd. She was too afraid to call for help. She claimed that I said, 'Let's sit on Jefferson's bed just so that we can say we did it,' and then I pushed her back on the heavy damask cover, a replica of the bedcovers Jefferson brought back from Paris with him, and it's true that I remember the feeling of the cover, heavy woven with lines of stylised flowers in silk thread. Underneath there was a more matter-of-fact contemporary mattress, and nothing more. And Gloria, as I remember it, was giggling as she pulled up her pleated skirt and slipped off her panties and I entered her. In my memory there was very little resistance, only a slippery and ardent welcome, made all the more exciting by the long delays and the sudden dangerous resolution. It would be customary to imagine that I came immediately, a teenage rite sanctified by tradition, but this is not true either. We spent a few, maybe three, vigorous minutes under the damask. I remember her complaining joyfully, that the mattress underneath her was tickling her. We had plenty of preparation for this moment. She moved purposefully. She uttered blissful noises while I half tried to quiet her. Then we quickly jumped out of bed, rearranged the covers and pulled on our clothes. (I was wearing black chinos, which I can verify from photographs in the yearbook.) She said, 'Thomas, you old devil, you,' to one of Jefferson's pictures in the entrance hall, where the Mandan robe hung.

That's how I remember it.

But last night after she had gone heavily to sleep, I lay awake feeling the overheated radiance of her body and listening to her heavy breathing. It was not the breathing of a seventeen-year-old, that's for sure, but something more sonorous. It's a puzzle why our breathing should take this laboured turn as we get older. As I listened to her, I imagined I heard in this tympany some of the struggles of her life. Although I was desperate to sleep myself, I could not. The music of her disappointments, the gentle two-note fluting, played loudly on my overstimulated senses. What I saw all too clearly was that there are a myriad of lives, an equal number of turnings which we could have lived. In the dry overheated room the skin on my face was flaking. I was tormented by these possibilities. Perhaps that is what is really meant by the immortality of the soul, the sense that your self has infinite possibilities and that they hang on a thread.

I lay and watched CNN with the volume very low until morning. Clinton was winning by a street, and in fact it seemed that he had passed this way – Detroit, Ann Arbor, Lansing – that very day. Dole was still trying to suggest that he would be able to summon up the old main street values of Henry Ford and Greenfield Village. Some chance. Still I could not sleep.

It may be true that I have treated the memory of Thomas Jefferson's bed with a lack of the appropriate reverence. I have congratulated myself many times on this feat; I've even told appreciative audiences at dinner parties about it when I've judged the moment to be right. Of course in the telling I've added a little colour: the backwoods high school, the rows of eager cheerleaders, the corny school trip, a few knowing remarks about Thomas Jefferson's slave mistresses, that sort of thing. This was not worthy. What I could never have envisaged – 'envisioned' as we say around here – was that I would be heading one day for the Wayne State Penitentiary to meet the killer of my purported offspring of that frolic, Scott Hollinger. A serial killer who has killed six women and bitten off their nipples, in some fantastic act of revenge for poor mothering. Oh God.

Sleep seemed to be an impossibility. Yet I must have fallen deeply asleep because by the time the vacuum cleaners began to scream in the hallway, Gloria was gone, leaving a note. The curlicued handwriting was the same as the writing in my yearbook, the 'Dan' done with a little flourish, and the Correction Services' telephone number underlined twice, in girlish emphasis. The PR man, who it seemed was eagerly looking forward to hearing from me, the prodigal returned from rainy old historic decrepit interesting England, was called Floyd Huskisson. Before setting out for the town of Holland to see Gary this morning I spoke to Floyd Huskisson, and he treated the matter with brisk and cheery openness. Of course the perpetrator had to agree, and he had to confirm that he had a message, but he didn't believe Hollinger was about to raise any objection, seeing as how he had spoken with two other victims' families. Both families, he added, had reported that they had grown from the experience.

Now I am tired. The Mandan robe is heavy. The tobacco smoke is like incense in church, inducing a spiritual defeatism. Gary is sitting Indian-style. I sink back with my head on a roll of hides and pelts. I am soon drifting off, hoping that I'll dream interesting and significant dreams because I feel guilty about not paying attention while Gary is communing with the spirits.

I don't dream but I wake confused and itchy and Gary is shaking me gently.

'You went right out there for near on an hour.'

'Yes. I'm sorry. I talked very late into the night with Gloria.'

'She's got a thing for you.'

'Do you think so?'

'To her you are the real thing. And then you left so suddenly.'

'Did she tell you she came to England to look for me?'

'Yes, I knew that, that's a long time ago.'

'Does everybody know?'

'I'm not sure about that. No, I'm not sure about that. Mom has made us something to eat. Are you hungry?'

I am, in that anxious way, from lack of sleep or excessive drinking, a compulsive need to restore some balance or make good some imagined depletion. Gary is smiling at me. His smile is indulgent, but also mad. His face is spotted with the Indian markings.

'While you were asleep I shot you with the migis,' he says. 'Don't worry, it's not harmful. I suppose in your church – you're an Episcopalian, right? – it's called a blessing, it's an Indian blessing.'

'In what way am I blessed?'

'We say *ki to no bi in ne he he*. This is what the migis has given us. It's a blessing against evil spirits and a protection against disease.'

'That can't be bad. Gary, when you say "shot", no injections are involved or any drugs?'

'No. No, Dan, trust me. The migis is our word for shells. These shells, which came from the great oceans, impart sacred knowledge. To be shot with a migis is symbolic. You can see why it is important to have back the scrolls, which passed down our migration routes for generations. They're not like road maps, more a kind of spiritual map, showing significant places. I went to Jerusalem when I was at Harvard, and I followed the Via Dolorosa. That is not historic or accurate but it has power, unbelievable spiritual power for Christians. It's the same with us.'

He sits very still watching to see how I am taking this information. Actually in my fuddled state I'm thinking that I would like to get out of this malodorous tent and sit down in the Delft kitchen amongst scenes of swing bridges and windmills and caged birds.

'Your mom still do that tuna bake?'

'How did you guess?'

To add to my confusion, it's almost dark outside. The week's snow has become crusty and it yields underfoot, with a crunch like breakfast cereal. Gary leads the way, tall, hunched, his long face locked downwards. His mother must be used to the spotty effect, white and green and red, across his forehead underneath the remains of the russet cow's-lick. While I'm having a piss a few moments later I see that I have a new band of spots on my forehead.

'Don't worry,' he says, 'it washes off real easy.'

8

In the Silent Night Memorial Chapel the words of 'Silent Night' are displayed on plaques, one hundred of them. The chapel is an exact replica of one in Oberndorf in Austria, where 'Silent Night' was first sung. Near by is an alpine village, which contains the greatest variety of crèches in America, and where the life-sized animals stand, heads lowered, around the infant. They have a rather alpine appearance, especially the cows, which look like the animals on packs of Swiss chocolate, too furry to survive the heat of the Judaean hills. The Virgin's shawl is of a distinctly baroque blue and the manger itself is full of plump Midwestern wheat stalks. Joseph stands to one side, under a hayrick, a little overwhelmed by the recent and unexpected arrival of three kings, wearing their gowns and kneeling. Under his crown, one of the kings has the unnaturally regular features of OJ Simpson. There are other details, cherubs and so on, which are copies of well-loved church decorations in those parts of Europe where they put on a good Christmas. You get the feeling that there they have the copyright on Christmas.

The front of the store looks like the entrance to a ski-lift in the Arlberg. There is a porte-cochère of fretworked wood, into which buses are driving to release ghostly streams of elderly people whose hair and clothes seem to have been toned down so that they are inoffensively pastel and pale. They trickle from the buses in thin, uncertain lines, pausing nervously to be sure they're going the right way, even though there is only one way, into the vast store behind. Viewed dispassionately, the twelve acres of the store are a bit like a warehouse, with a phoney alpine frontage of wooden slats, but the Christmas music plays cheerfully and there are nice touches, like the elaborate lamps with flickering realistic gas flames. I have seen something similar in Innsbruck.

I promised to pick Gloria up from work. I made this promise just before she made her accusation. Shortly after, she was asleep, the sleep of the just, while I lay beside her. Now as I approach the entrance to the Christmas superstore, I see that lying next to someone for a night is an extraordinary intimacy: asleep we are so helpless and the little noises and emissions we produce are evidence that the immortal soul lives in an imperfectly functioning human sac. And it's the bodily imperfections and decay which lead us to desire a permanence of the human essence. If I understand Gary right, the human spirit flits between worlds, between the sky and the earth, between this world and the spirit world. The Indians need points of contact, graves, in order to communicate with their ancestors and relations. They need their scrolls, too, incised on birchbark, which was the papyrus of the Indian world, to guide them in their journeys in and out of other worlds. There is one scroll in particular which Gary wishes me to recover. There may be more. Incidentally he would also like any news I can give him on the location of the King's Broad Axe, an immense wampum belt given to Tecumseh and his followers by the Crown to encourage them in their resistance to the Americans, who were arriving daily. I have seen a painting showing Daniel Boone leading the settlers through the Cumberland Gap. The look on the faces of these newcomers is not unlike the look on the faces of the senior citizens, approaching the entrance of Bronner's, nervous but steeled. I edge politely through the lines of elderly people.

The interior of the store is a wonder. The Austrians and the Swiss, the Tyrolean Italians and the Bavarians can't compete with this. Their little dinky Christmasses may be the inspiration, but this bears the same relation to their version of the festivities as the Statue of Liberty bears to a roadside shrine. This is the World Series of Christmas.

I move among the aisles and walkways, which are a scented, winking, shimmering, crooning riot of Christmas. There is a whole section devoted to ribbons and bindings. Somewhere people must be manufacturing ribbons in every colour and sheen and material known to man. There are huge red satin ribbons, pre-tied into bows, and there are ribbons which have continuous hieroglyphs of reindeers and sleighs and snowmen. There are ribbons in silk and nylon and every known sort of fibre; there are three hundred varieties of string, from miniature bellropes to silken flax; and there are aisles of snow domes, one the size of a small igloo in which a family of Eastern European peasant farmers is lost every other minute in a violent blizzard, only to re-emerge apple-cheeked and cheerful after a few anxious moments. The little boy, the son of the house, is about to throw a snowball for a large gambolling dog of unfamiliar breed; just as you think the snowball will be launched, the blizzard appears from behind some nicely triangular mountains and obliterates the landscape. It is priced at $5,600. The costume department demonstrates, for those interested in such matters, the cultural variations of Christmas. As well as the traditional beard and red suit trimmed with fur, there are old men in blue tunics, rows of Santa Lucia dresses of virginal whiteness and St Sylvestre (who has to be wakened every New Year) outfits; there are coalsacks for St Niklaus and brass bells and comfortable boots of rustic materials, and a variety of belts, crowns of candles, as well as more specialised portable accessories for Greek and Russian Orthodox Christmasses. These to me are a little sinister.

I am scouting in this vast illusion. People today love these huge, controlled artificial spaces. When I was a boy we used to go down to Detroit to see the Lions play out in the open air. It often snowed. Now the whole thing takes place inside the Silverdome, not unlike a snow dome, except that the snow falls outside. In these places the conditions are always perfect, just as in here it is always Christmas. The air is laden with spruce and fur and pine and the music is upbeat and festive with perhaps a little hint of fascism in the brass. You won't hear gangster rap in here, nor will the old people ghosting about be reminded of the divided America of the big cities. Even the few elderly black people wandering about appear to have taken on the inoffensive and utterly nondescript look of their white age-mates. Also, their skin is discolouring, becoming in patches a sort of bruised mustard colour, the colour of mushrooms a day or two old.

Everywhere there are women employees in dirndls and men in white kneesocks and braces. The fact that they all appear to speak the flat local English does not disturb the seasonal illusion. To the visitors, this is probably better than the Alps. There are no language, currency, toilet or culinary problems. I see that Americans have no inhibitions about living in the present, as my father said. The past happened at another time.

Gloria's department is dominated by a very tall centrepiece, a sixty-foot tree, hung with red ribbons and silver boxes and bundles of spices, vanilla pods and sticks of cinnamon. The lights on the tree look like real candles at first sight, until you see that there is an unnatural regularity in their flickering. Around the base of the tree are beautifully wrapped gift boxes. I see Gloria dealing with a party of women with name tags. She's explaining something to them soundlessly; her kind eyes and her smile, though housed now in a more fleshy face, are startlingly the same. I wonder what Belinda looked like. I feel strongly now the sense of other worlds, worlds which I will never know. I feel an aching sadness about Belinda amongst the pine resins and cinnamon smells and the Christmas music. Whatever the truth about her, I have been foolish enough to imagine that life here went into mothballs when I left, a sort of provincial nothingness. Instead it has been going on ritually, perversely, just as full of human meaning as anything I have been up to.

There she stands, the cheerleader whom I had loved, in a way, and whom I had almost forgotten, written out of my story. My story. We're all writing our stories in some fashion. The whole world is now seeing itself as a character in the cosmic drama. And yet, conscious as you are of the absurdity of this, you can't escape.

Gloria opens a box of deep-red glass balls. From here they look to me like persimmons. As she holds one up for inspection by the party of pale seniors, she sees me watching her and gives me a little wave with her free hand. Two old ladies look round in my direction. Gloria has told me that she has a 'friend' at the store and I scan the *faux-alpinistes* in their white stockings to see if I can identify this person. Could it be that man over there busying himself with the nutcracker display? Or that one, older but with a boyish fringe, wrapping some crystal Steuben angels? Gloria holds up her hand, fingers spread: five minutes. She does it in a way that suggests intimacy, a shared semaphore. And I feel myself asking: how well do I know her? Who is this person I've spent the night with? And Gary Pale Eagle, who was once my friend, what has he become? And what have I become, with my white house, and my carefully nurtured life which now seems so self-regarding? As insubstantial as the wampum belt that Gary has asked me to find, the King's Broad Axe. It was supposed to cut a swathe through the Americans who were advancing to plant their homesteads and their churches and their Christmas wonderlands. The wampum belt was nothing but shells; it was a weapon of the mind only. The Indians must have placed great value on the power of natural objects, and I see that Gary shares this faith, with his otter medicine bag and the bear-claw necklace he has given me.

Now Gloria is gently directing one of the old folk away, with a light pressure on the arm. They are talking about her date. I remember so clearly the urgency of the date; everyone needed to have a date. Even girls who couldn't stand the boy they were dating would continue just because of the compelling nature of the words: *I've got a date.* I haven't used the phrase for twenty years at least. I try it out on Gloria, fresh-aproned, eyes like Delftware, as she advances towards me: *I have a date.*

Actually we're double-dating. Duane Buta and Karen Petersen, who was Karen Wardie, one a widower, one divorced, are going to join us at Willi's German Sausage Haus, where authentic German sausages are served, Gloria says. Duane and Karen were unable to attend the reunion and they're apparently keen to see me again.

'Good day?' I ask.

'Can't complain. I wanted to say goodbye, but you were really crashed out.'

128

'No problem.'

'I'll just get my coat and freshen up a little and I'll be right there by the south check-outs.'

The check-outs are lined with green and red felt. The warehouse roofing above them is hung with gift stockings and reindeer and giant crackers. It reminds me of the delicatessen, Fratelli Camisa, near the agency in Soho, where I used to buy olives and polenta and crumbling slabs of Parmesan: the roof was hung with mortadella and hams and those Italian cakes which are quickly recycled at Christmas: the boxes are festive but the contents are too light and dry, vanilla-scented sawdust.

As I wait I wonder if I could ever live out here again, so far from the things which make cities attractive: the hopeful new enterprises and the old established, the texture of the buildings, the brick-by-brick, stone-by-stone accumulation of striving, the smudges of human breath and blood, the unexpected vistas; the sense that a city, New York or London, for example, is like a glacier inching inexorably forwards compelled by unseen forces. And in cities you have real and present things to think about: out here you probably have to worry about far-off things like the Federal Government and the Chinese. Mind you, Flint has had its problems, but they're mainly the problems of apathy unleavened by human genius and mad folly. Gene took me through the 'upscale' part of Flint on the way home the other day: clustered around an art gallery and a few prep schools were streets of authentic mansions. Gene lives just at the edge of this cultural haven, just where the houses are beginning to subside into more familiar suburban dimensions. He takes personal pride in the area. I couldn't tell him that it all looked faintly ridiculous, with the imperial eagle gateways and leaded baronial windows and eclectic statuary and strategically placed wrought-iron benches. And there is the clear message that European artefacts by their nature are exclusive. These classy things are meant to repel the overweight people with their junk cars full of paper cups, the bumpers plastered with redneck slogans, their radios turned to moronic chat shows, those people who are unable to tell travertine from Formica or Palladio from plywood. The rich, and white, citizens are pulling up the cultural drawbridge to the sound of classical music.

Gloria is wearing a long coat trimmed at the cuffs with fur. I wonder if it is her best coat, one she thinks is romantic. I kiss her on both cheeks.

'Très chic,' she says.

'We were in French together.'

'You were the only boy.'

Her skin is warm and smells faintly of resin.

'What have you got on your face?' she asks.

'It's Gary's Indian stuff.'

'Oh.'

'Shall we take my car?' I ask.

'No,' she says. 'We shall walk. I want you to see the Christmas tree lane and the old Swiss bridge.'

She takes my arm and we stroll, first across the immense carpark (parking for three thousand cars) and then through the avenue of Christmas trees, lit against the blank dark sky, which I think is fetching more snow from its depths, in a thousand shocks and pinpricks and starbursts of electric light.

'Do you remember Edison's lab?' I ask.

'You've got sex on the brain,' she says cheerfully.

But it's not sex I have on the brain. I am in the grip of a compulsion to allow my past self some air and light, as though it could quickly develop in different ways, as though it could swell, and I could be going to Willi's Sausage Haus not as a slightly ill-at-ease visitor but as the person I would have been if I had never left. I wonder if this sort of wild thinking is the result of Gary's migis, the traces still lingering near my ears. As we clatter across the wooden enclosed Swiss bridge which spans the Cass River, it occurs to me that Gary may have left his old self behind, like a hermit crab moving on, in a similar fashion.

'The bridge was imported piece by piece from a town near Zurich, Switzerland,' Gloria says.

'It's beautiful. It's like that bridge in the Henry Ford Museum, near the Cape Cod windmill. Do you remember that?'

'My, you do have sex on the brain.'

We are walking across the main street, her hand linked to my forearm, which I'm carrying like a shotgun, when I hear a voice calling: 'Dan, Dan, how are you, old cocksucker?'

'It's Duane,' Gloria says. 'Ignore him. He's become kinda hyper since Sheree died.'

'Hey, Dan, you look just fine. Except you look like you got chicken pox or something.'

I wipe my face with my sleeve.

'No, no, it's not chicken pox. I'll explain later,' I say.

'How are you, you old snake-oil salesman?'

'I'm fine. How the hell are you?' I say, trying to sound convincingly upbeat.

'Gloria told you, Sheree passed away, but you know you just got to pick yourself up. Hey buddy, how comes you ran away and never even sent a change of address card?'

131

'It's not that simple. But the last couple of days I have been asking myself that question, or something similar anyway.'

Duane is wearing a sheepskin jacket and a leather hat with earflaps. I recalled him only as a boy who wanted to go to Vietnam but now, in the light of Willi's Sausage Haus, where we stand for a moment assaulted by the smell of bratwurst, I recognise him. His face has a foetal appearance, a near-albino paleness which, with the freeing up of the Eastern Bloc states, I recognise as Ukrainian. Back then the name meant nothing. Again I imagine I see all the streams of European migration in those faces, heading out from the Urals and the Carpathians and the Black Forest and the fjords.

'There's Karen,' says Gloria, just as we are entering the restaurant.

A Cherokee is pulling into a parking lot. Karen was the head cheerleader and the homecoming queen, an object of desire, but she was already going with a recent graduate, a football star at Michigan State who occasionally paid lordly visits to our parties. Now they're divorced. He left her for a young woman in his law office in East Lansing and Karen has come back to live near home. She parks the Cherokee and bounds over, tall and energetic. I expect her to do a cartwheel, and hope to see those pants again. She seizes my hand and holds it while our cheeks touch.

'Well, Dan, a little older but no wiser, I'll bet.'

'Wise enough to get the fuck outa here,' says Duane zestfully. 'Let's go and eat sausage, big time.'

He removes his leather cap and I see that his hair is short and grizzled, cut marine style, so that he looks like a younger version of Demanjuk, the camp trusty tried in Jerusalem. These features have a kind of potato-dumpling look, an emptiness

that movies have made us think of as sinister. In the same
way English people are now seen as devious and duplicitous in
Hollywood movies.

Willi's Sausage Haus is full. We have to stand for a few
minutes by the bar drinking steins of beer, with lids of pewter.

'I just love this place,' says Karen. 'It is so European.'

And I remember how enthusiastic she always was. I now see
that her eyes are bulging slightly, as though she has thyroid
problems. Already in these few days I have scanned too many
faces trying to see the sense in the passage of time and the
turnings we have made. Why should I have this hope? There is
no sense, but I feel, with the German weissbier in my veins, as
though I have wilfully turned my eyes away from the richness of
life – American life – and passed my life in a meaningless series
of Tourette tics and echolalia.

At Duane's insistence I quickly have another beer.

'You remember that bottle of vodka we drank in DC?' he
asks.

'Oh yes. Where were we?'

'On the bus from Montibello to DC.'

'Monticello.'

'That's it, Monticello. You always was a kinda know-all typa
guy. Anyways, there we are in a bus drunk as a coupla skunks,
and Gloria's sitting quietly crying her eyes out in the back of
the bus. I asked you what her problem was, and you said "She's
just had sex with a founding father." I never forgot that.'

I couldn't have said that. Gloria is talking to Karen, old, old
friends, but still competitive. They glance at me for a moment.

'Then the next day when that guide at Mount Vernon said,
"Here's where George Washington threw a silver dollar across the

Potomac" – it's about a mile wide – you said, "Shows a dollar went a lot fucking further in those days." Everybody heard, including Mr Zabruder. You were a bundla laughs. You've become kinda serious now.'

Is it true that Gloria was crying all the way from Richmond County? Could I be wrong about the lovemaking too, which over the years has been for me a talisman, an innocent memory full of charm?

Mercifully our table is ready before Duane can, in his excitable way, reveal any more of my failings to me. We order sausages and schnitzel and potatoes and salad and the selection of German mustards; I see the weisswurst and bratwurst, fat and glistening and lightly scored by the grill. Here the waitresses also dress in Bavarian style. As they lean forward to place more beer on our table, Duane gives me a significant look.

'Whaddya think of those?' he asks.

'Jesus, Duane, can't you ever grow up?' asks Karen.

'I sure hope not.'

'You look a little out of it,' says Gloria sympathetically.

'I had a hard day's induction with Gary.'

'What do the red spots mean?'

'Can you still see them?'

'Yeah, in a certain light, just by your ears.'

'They mean knowledge.'

'What kinda knowledge?'

'I can't be sure. Gloria, did you mean what you said last night about Jefferson's bed?'

'I did, but it was a long time ago.'

The sausages and schnitzels arrive.

'Looks like Slick Willy's going to get back in,' says Karen brightly.

'Yeah, because dumb women like him. Strange thing, ain't it, that women like this kind of guy. For myself, I don't see him as a real Democrat, not a Reuther type of Democrat. This state would still be where it was if the Democrats hadn't sold out.'

'Jesus, Duane, put a sock in it. Lighten up. Reuther and his pals are Jurassic. History. The UAW finished Flint. End of story. Clinton's pragmatic.'

'Pragmatic? What kind of a word is that for a cheerleader?'

'Duane, fuck off, will you.'

This exchange is no more than slightly weary banter. Around us the old in their apologetic clothes are eating carefully as though they expect to find lead shot in their sausages, while the boisterous sturdy young are becoming louder. Their faces are very familiar to me, the faces of the loggers and beet farmers who first came here in the last century and hardly noticed the fleeting Indians. To me these faces have the appearance of contentment, agrarian in origin.

Duane is becoming drunk quickly. He, like Gene, wants me to know that it hasn't been all hayrides and chicken dinners here.

'You Europeans,' (he pronounces this 'Yurpeens') 'don't seem to realise that out here in the sticks we're still producing half the world's goods — cars and much more. Take Dow, there's forty different plants right there in the Thumb, producing everything from Saran Wrap to latex for your basic johnnies. We don't just produce gas guzzlers. Yes, please, honey, bring me another dunkel. Look at the knockers on that.'

I have already glanced her way as she leans forward to pick up the empties.

'Try to think of him as harmlessly retarded,' says Gloria quickly. 'Women become a little desperate, you know. Karen sees that he's a kinda numbnuts but, hey, she's the homecoming queen. Someone's got to pay court, for the moment anyway. You know what I'm saying? He's filling the gap.'

The sausages are slippery. I wonder what they do to the meat in them to produce this even pink and white sponginess. Gloria is licking her fingers, where traces of mild German mustard are visible.

'Did you speak to the PR guy?' she asks, 'at the prison?'

'Yes. He says he'll ask the perpetrator if it's okay for me to come and see him.'

'That's bull, actually. They have ways of making them agree. You know, like "How badly do you want to have the television amenity next week?" and so on. He's just saying that. Here, I have a picture for you.'

She gives me a small photograph of Belinda. Gloria's face in the German warmth, the bustle of the waitresses, the splutter of sausages on the grill — even the brass band music radiates heat — is glistening. I must do what I can to help her. If I can, I will also perform a small task for Gary. I look at Belinda. She is wearing a mortar board and a gown, holding her graduation scroll. Her face has that smile that graduation conveys, a suppressed pride. Her eyes are deeply set in her head, so that they are not picking up the photographer's light. I peer at the picture apprehensively to see if I can find any traces of myself in there. I cannot.

Duane is drunk. Maybe I am too, because I feel a sudden elation, a surging in the blood, water slopping in a pail; it may be the drink, or it may be the migis.

9

Jack Kervorkian is pictured in the *Flint Journal,* packing his car before he sets out on a mission to end a life. In his car — it looks like a Passat — he has cylinders of carbon monoxide and bottles of potassium chloride. The patient has Lou Gehrig's Disease, and does not want to live a moment longer. It is unfortunate that Dr Kervorkian looks so sinister. The paper quotes one of his opponents as saying that he is suffering from a form of monomania: there is a lot more to being a doctor than helping people die, yet Kervorkian appears to think that euthanasia is the whole purpose of medicine, in the same way that Spaniards believe that the whole purpose of a fighting bull's life is death in the corrida. Kervorkian is looking back over his shoulder at the photographer nervously. Reading the report I see that his notoriety has inspired some perverse pride in Michiganders: he is a world figure, and celebrity, however obtained, is better than obscurity.

Below, the thin life of the hotel is relayed to me in snatches of Muzak and p.a. announcements and the whack of the Coca-Cola machine up the hall.

Outside fresh snow has fallen: the carpark is arctic. It was falling last night as we left Willi's Sausage Haus and said our goodbyes at the covered wooden bridge. Duane tried to piss over the side. Gloria and I hurried on, our faces bent against the snowflakes. I wondered what sort of domestic recrimination was waiting for Duane when he and Karen reached home. She has moved into a small duplex, built behind the site of the Farmers' Market in Hollybush, and Duane was halfway moved in. Men and women who have been round the track once or twice have a sense of being ridiculous. They are carrying injuries, as they say in the sports pages, but they are injuries to the self-esteem, no less visible. By the time the strudel arrived – buried under what the waiter called *Schlagsahne* – cream like shaving foam – Karen had been to the rest-room twice, accompanied by Gloria, to regain her shaky composure. I wondered what they said in there, what pep talks were handed out. During the second hiatus, Duane told me that he had lusted after Karen all his life and now at the moment critique he couldn't get it up. But when Karen returned, chirpy and upbeat, Duane renewed his dialogue with the surprisingly tolerant waitresses.

Gloria drove off into the night and the thickening blizzard. I had expected her to want to come back to the hotel with me and I was dreading it. But when she left me in the snow, without an explanation, I felt abandoned. I promised her again that I would go to the prison to receive the message, whatever that might be. The Christmas trees were winking in the snow and their boughs were heavy; the music from the Silent Night Chapel was stilled. The carpark was vast and my car stood isolated and crusted. I had the sensation then, which still lingers this morning, that the self is a sort of tyranny, the burden of being human. The burden is the belief that we are meant to be more than what we find.

Somos màs was a rallying cry in Chile under repression. *We are more than this.* You could say, *there must be more than this.* Increasingly, Stephanie's conversation had been about her need to grow and develop. Her exercising and her diets, involving theories about food combinations, had irritated me for months. But of course they were only the symptons: her self was troubled and trammelled. I wished she would put it in plain English. Finally she did, in the form of an ultimatum.

As Gloria left in her nondescript car, made even more anonymous by its cladding of snow, and I walked across the empty snowfield to mine, I had a powerful urge to call Stephanie and see if we could start again. But there are no new beginnings in this way: too much had been said, too many accusations had been made. And then there was the sexual business, itself a tyranny, a web of the physical and the imagined, constraining and urging and finally existing only as a reproach. It was this failure of the imagination that she wanted to replace with marriage and motherhood because they would have provided a vindication for what otherwise was wasted time. And yet for me, our early years together were ecstatic, far from wasted. As I struggled to get the keys into the frozen lock, I saw how unfair I had been to her. What I had loved – her wild, slightly soiled sexual avidity – was only one aspect of her life and I had cruelly rejected any attempts she made to reveal the others. And it was because I was a big cheese in advertising and because Stephanie was the sort of woman I thought I should be seen with. I had known these facts all along the way. Now they seemed shameful. And now Gloria, too, was trying to see the hidden purpose in what we had done.

When I finally managed to open the door (I can suffer moments of Hulot-like ineptitude), my face and hands were aching. This raw cold, this lung-searing cold, was frightening. How had the Indians lived through these winters out there in their lodges?

Across the vast Christmas carpark, behind the Silent Night Chapel, I heard their chant, *ka wi ka da an ne we was si nan*, which Gary said was the call to the spirits that never failed. And then I heard the chorus, *he-he-he-he — yo*, blown on the wind, thin and desperate, a hopeless plea.

The snow on the windscreen refused to budge. It had become a frozen bubble-wrap. I turned on the radio and heard Bruce Springsteen singing 'On the Streets of Philadelphia'; I thought that we are all calling to the spirits, in our own way.

And now breakfast arrives in that brisk, aggressively cheery manner, the croissant and blueberry bran muffin, cohabiting on the plate, the vacuum flask of inoffensive coffee, the juice wearing its paper hat. The phone rings.

'Hello.'

'Mr Silas?'

'Yes.'

'It's the Michigan Correctional Department. I'm Lindi Holman, assistant to the public affairs officer.'

'Oh yes, hello.'

'We have spoken with the perpetrator, Mr Hollinger, and he has agreed to see you.'

'Oh, good.'

'Can you come over this afternoon?'

Good God. This afternoon. I was thinking in terms of a return visit in a few months.

'All right,' I say. 'What time?'

'Come around two p.m. sir. It takes a few minutes to complete the formalities. Could you tell me now if you are prepared to talk to Mr Hollinger without a guard present? He will be shackled?'

'Yes, I am.'

'Would you mind bringing some ID sir, your passport or a driving licence containing your photograph?'

'Sure. Fine.'

'Well that's all then. Come to the visitor center and we'll take care of you. Ask for me, Lindi Holman.'

'Thanks Lindi.'

'You're welcome, sir. Goodbye.'

Knowledge comes from the heart.

My heart is billowing erratically. I call Gary to tell him I won't be visiting, as planned. His mother answers.

'How are you, Dan?'

'I'm fine. But I have to go to Harrison today.'

'Gary will be disappointed not to see you. He was looking forward to it.'

'I'm sorry, but I'll come again as soon as I can.'

'All right. Your return after all these years has been very good for him. I must go now. Come again as soon as you are ready.'

'May I speak to him?'

'Not just at the moment. Senator Dole is making a fool of himself, don't you think? Goodbye.'

The iceberg mother. Does she ever wonder what Gary is thinking? She seems to treat him as she always did, distant and impersonal, as though she is observing him through plate glass. I am thinking of those old movies where the father arrives at the maternity hospital and is shown his wife and newborn baby through a window, after they had been arranged on the bed. He then goes to the bar and buys his friends a cigar.

Knowledge comes from the heart.

If this is so, we can only gain wisdom — if we can gain wisdom, which is not proven — by deliberately ignoring the self. But it is impossible to do this. So it must be impossible to make a meaningful decision to rely on the heart only, both because our self and our emotions are one and the same and because, by making this decision, we are immediately subverting our own intention of relying on the heart's message. How we used to enjoy this kind of argument over in my tutor's chilly dog-eared rooms. He was very fond of the verification principle, but I couldn't see then what it could mean in real life.

Perhaps Stephanie's belief that parenthood would be an epiphany for us has some truth in it; because children are a wholly new fact in your life — everyone says — which quickly outgrows any previously laid plans. It might well lead to new understanding, to an enforced selflessness. Perhaps visiting the killer of my daughter — if she was my daughter — will lead to new understanding, a new connectedness with events. Last night one of the mock-German waitresses, talking to another girl just by the toilets as I walked by was saying, 'I like her, but she's kinda selfish.' And I have noticed that 'selfish' now means self-obsessed.

I dress quickly and call Gene's office.

'He's in a meeting right now.'

'Can you tell him Mr Silas wants to speak to him?'

'I'll try and pass a message to him. He's with a client.'

'Okay. Tell him I'm at the hotel.'

Within a few minutes Gene calls back. His voice is cheerful but wary. He has a load to carry; he's a figure in the community.

'Hey, Dan, what's up?'

'I'm going to the penitentiary to see this guy Hollinger.'

'Jesus, that does not sound like a very good idea to me.'

'Gloria wants me to.'

'I don't know, Dan. What's the point? I mean what is the bastard going to tell you? That he liked chewing the tits off young girls, that he wasn't breast fed, that he is an Anthony Hopkins fan? Don't do it Dan.'

'I've got to now. In a strange way I'm looking forward to it.'

'Are you crazy? Listen, Dan, let me give it to you straight, as I see it. Belinda was Fred Larssen's daughter. Fred accepted her totally. And Gloria, despite all that cheesy cheerleader and glee-club stuff, screwed other people before – and after – you, Dan. You know that. You have no responsibility beyond that of any old friend. That's what I was trying to tell you the other night. If you have got some other agenda of your own, forget it. This Hollinger is a standard sicko; he should have been strangled at birth. Gloria has been seeing this psychotherapist guy, and he's probably told her that her daughter had a message for her or some crap like that. This country's going nuts, Dan. Keep out of this mess. Listen, I've got a client waiting in reception. Call me around lunchtime.'

But now I am heading towards the penitentiary in Harrison, Wayne County. In a few days I have become familiar with the landscape again; the brutality of the winter gives the journey a seamlessness as if there are no fences and fields or sidewalks, just this broad, grey-white ribbon of road through a wilderness of snow. Limbaugh is complaining about the teaching of history. He says that the liberals are giving the message that our country is inherently evil; everyone who was thought to be a hero was in fact evil: 'That's right folks. That's what we're doing to history today.' There seems to me some basis for his fears, namely that heroism is historical selectivity, endorsement for a point of view. I remember civics lessons when we learnt about how a bill becomes a law and about presidents and their achievements, but nothing about lobbyists, influence salesmen and campaign funding. And both Thomas Jefferson and Henry Ford have taken a pasting. Limbaugh then turns to the subject of Clinton again, and I switch stations. I wonder if Jack Kervorkian is also driving through this, just like any other man going off to work; instead of ladders or lawnmowers or plumbing equipment in the back of his car, he has sinister cylinders and phials.

Somewhere in Ohio a doctor has been jailed for feeding rat poison to his colleagues. The poison contained arsenic. He administered it in Extra Spicy Kentucky Fried Chicken.

What am I expecting from Hollinger? Nothing that will be comforting for Gloria, but perhaps something that will grant me some knowledge of the desirable, unconscious sort.

The houses begin to thicken as the highway heads south. I take the off-ramp, as directed towards the town of Harrison. I am tempted to keep on. Why not? It's a time-honoured tradition in America, driving on, avoiding trouble, starting again, losing yourself in the vastness. The seductive vastness. The turn-off for the penitentiary appears too suddenly out of flat scrub. I turn and brake fast and for a moment I feel the car sliding, suddenly free of my control, before the wheels hit something substantial and I move cautiously down a long straight road to the first perimeter fence. *State of Michigan, Department of Correction, State Penitentiary, Harrison Facility.* Does anybody believe in correction and penitence any longer? Perfectability is your own responsibility now, in your chosen fashion. You are your own authority.

They are expecting me. At the touch of a button a huge gate opens and I am confined in a small area between fences. The woman officer at the desk has a gun at her belt. She is straining the permanently pressed fawn pants with thighs and buttocks, that are as round and solid as the hams which hang from the roof of the Italian deli in Soho. Her manner is friendly and girlish. She looks like a Czech tennis player gone to seed; her hair is fine wood shavings; her cheekbones are high and her eyes so widely spaced that there is an alarming prairie above the base of her nose. She signs me in by tapping my name into a computer. The second set of enormous gates rolls open.

The penitentiary is a low building spreading flat across the snowfields, more like a silicon-chip estate than the traditional prison. As I approach the third gate, it slides open automatically and I follow the signs to my parking space.

The cordon sanitaire around the prison is empty of life and excessively, puritanically, unadorned; just the bare brickwork of the reception block and the long, featureless outer wall. The place, set in flat farmland, gives off a dull thrum of despair. Now I see that there are two stands of high-voltage wire on top of the wall, decorated with a bright and jaunty skull and crossbones.

I walk to the reception. My legs feel stiff and unwilling. Gloria, Gloria. What have you asked me to do? I long for my study, with its nicely aged carpet and the dog asleep on the old leather armchair. I want to bury my face in his plumpness and smell his fragrant dogginess. I am breathing too quickly. I wonder how I look. Before I left my room I put on a silk tie and a soft tweed jacket. It seemed to me that I should demonstrate a certain worldliness to Scott Hollinger, as I received his message. I am merely an ambassador. Now I wonder if I would not have been better off in sneakers and a fleece, more populist clothes. My mind is extremely volatile. This man has done unspeakable things; he may be angered by my appearance. He may be angered by my visit. I know next to nothing about Belinda, but I must ask him how she died. How will he know which one I am talking about? Presumably he and his victims did not exchange names and addresses. I have the photograph. I check my pocket. Passport. Photograph.

'Hi, I'm Lindi Holman.'

'Hello.'

She is dressed in a grey business suit with large shoulders and a shiny blouse underneath. She has bold hair, elaborately curled, framing a small voracious face, emphasising the carnivore's mouth.

'I just need to enter some details. Come this way please, Mr Silas.'

In a small office, completely bare except for a poster advertising an exhibition at the Henry Ford Museum called *The Automobile and American Life*, she sits at a computer and types. It has large, heavy keys, which she hits with a loud thwack.

'All done. Now I have to asks you a coupla questions. Ready to proceed?'

'Yes.'

'Do you want a rest-room stop or a cup of coffee before we begin?'

'Both.'

'Okay. Rest-room's just along the hall, I'll get the coffee. How do you take it?'

I have difficulty peeing. My bladder seems to be constricted.

'Right, well, we give you a few pointers. You will meet the perpetrator in a special interview room. He will already be there, shackled, so there is no danger. You can spend up to forty minutes talking with him. Water and coffee are available. You may take notes, but you must not take any recording device into the room. Do you have any such amenity?'

'No.'

'An officer will be watching through a two-way glass during the interview. If you are nervous or would wish to take a break, signal to the officer by holding your hand up like this.'

She demonstrates. Her hand is raised level with her head, the palm turned to the front.

'The perpetrator, Mr Hollinger, has shown no signs of violence since his sentence. Never the less we must ask you to stay on your side of the table, where he would be unable to reach you. Are you ready now?'

'Yes. I hope so.'

I stand up.

'Not yet sir, I will call through.'

She picks up a chunky grey phone. I sit down again.

'It takes approximately five minutes.'

She speaks into the phone: 'Visitor ready. Okay. Yup.'

I drink my coffee. It has that familar taste of metal containers and Styrofoam. For a moment we are both silent.

'Were you close to your daughter, Mr Silas?'

'Not physically. I lived in England. But emotionally, yes.'

'I love Londin,' she says. 'It's real ...' she searches for an adjective for a second; 'it's real intrestin'.'

The phone rings.

'He's there. You ready, sir?'

We stand and I follow her out of the room; her hips are lean and her legs below the skirt are alarmingly thin and straight, so that it is hard to imagine how she can walk. On one ankle she wears a gold chain. I try to follow very calmly, but I feel as if I am shambling. Her hair from behind is magnificent, coppery and wavy like a show horse's mane. The corridor is long, built of plain blocks which were fashionable for a while with architects, who valued their guileless industrial texture. *Tick-tack-tick-tack*. Her red shoes make different notes on the floor. There is no sign of prisoners nor sounds of prison life. Somewhere those squat people, Hispanics with short, bulbous calves, and muscular black guys and tattooed white men with lank hair, are playing pool and watching television or working out; but their activities are utterly, utterly silent, expunged.

'This way, please.'

Doors, each with a number, face us now at a junction. This must be where the outside world finally meets the cons, the foreshore, where they emerge from the deep. I was once a juror and I wondered what it was like to be objectified. *Stand. Sit. Go down there. Stand. Wait, while I unlock the door. Hold out your hands. Go in. Stand while the judge passes sentence. Say nothing.* As a juror, I scanned the defendants closely for human signs. One seemed to be suffering convulsions of humiliation. Most were passive, one or two were cocky, as if just to have been the cause for all of us stiffs to assemble was some feat.

We enter one of the rooms. It is locked behind us. Lindi Holman asks me if I am ready.

'Yes.'

Ahead of us is another door.

'Okay. I will open the door now and introduce you.'

She knocks. A guard opens the door from the inside.

'This is Mr Daniel Silas,' she says. 'This is Mr Scott Hollinger.'

Already sitting at the table is a man of about thirty-five, with flat, dead hair and aviator's glasses. He is wearing a vee-necked green shirt, like a doctor in an operating theatre, and his reddish-blond chest hairs are poking out above the vee. His hands are on the table, but they are held together by manacles, to which a chain is attached. The chain leads down below the table.

'All right sir?' asks the guard.

He is a very broad man. The rolls of fat around his waist lap over the top of his belt. He points to the chair opposite Hollinger.

'You may sit, sir.'

'Thank you.'

'I'll see you again on your way out, Mr Silas,' says Lindi Holman.

'Fine. Thank you.'

Hollinger is looking at me. His gaze is steady, but curiously unfocused. Traces of severe teenage acne are pitted across his cheeks.

'I'll be there sir, behind that window,' says the guard.

'Thank you.'

'I'm Scott Hollinger,' says the prisoner when the guard has gone. He attempts a serious, business-like smile. 'What can I do for you today, sir?'

'My ... my, the mother of my girl, Belinda Larssen, wanted me to talk to you, to put her mind at rest, about whether she suffered ...'

I am holding her picture.

'Shoot. Ask away. I got nothing but time.'

He leans forward helpfully, and I lean back. His breath is not good; it reeks of confinement and idleness.

'Your lawyer said you had some message for Belinda's mother?'

'He said that? What an asshole. Can I look at that picture of her, sorry to say this, but to remind me, know what I'm saying?'

I place the picture of Belinda on the table in front of us. He reaches out with his manacled hands and draws it closer to him. His hands have thick blond hairs on them. He studies the picture. His eyes seem to be straining so that his face becomes lined. He begins to breathe more quickly and audibly.

'What's your question?'

'What did you want to tell her mother, that's my question?'

'Everyone is a god who has the freedom to create his own truth,' he says. He looks at me, smiling contentedly.

I feel anger rising. It's uncontrollable, like the vomit caused by food poisoning. I gaze at his eyes, slightly magnified by the glasses. They are moist, fixed on Belinda's graduation photograph which I too have looked at closely.

'What did you say?'

'In life, Mr Silas, I have found that you must only accept what rings true to your own self.'

'What does that mean, exactly?'

'It means what you want it to mean. Che sarà, sarà.'

He reaches down below the table. The picture is lying flat

150

now, some way over his side of the line. I can see the top of Belinda's mortar board.

The chain on his amulets begins to jingle. I watch his face in horror. He's staring at the picture, but I don't dare snatch it away.

'No sir, she didn't suffer. I fucked her good. I don't remember her complaining. Her last words were, fuck me harder next time. Your daughter is one hot little cumslut, sir.'

I jump up, grab my chair to hit him, to kill him; I am gulping for air, and sobbing. But before I can bring it up the guard is there. He gets between us and grabs Hollinger by the face with one hand. Hollinger smiles, even as his face is being twisted out of shape.

'When they abolished the death penalty in this state they made a big mistake, you piece of shit,' says the guard.

He turns to me. I am standing, still holding the back of the chair.

'I'm real sorry sir. I'm sorry you came all the way from England to see this scumbag.'

I try to move but I cannot. The guard reaches for the photograph, and hands it to me.

'Great necktie,' says Hollinger, as the guard leads me to the door. 'Nice coat.'

10

Henry Ford's Greenfield Village is almost deserted. It's too cold for school parties and it's late. The train is not running. I walk out in the direction of Edison's laboratory, but stop and enter the Wilbur and Orville Wright birthplace. An elderly man in a checked shirt is sitting there. For a moment I think he may be a relative of the Wrights, but of course it cannot be. He seems surprised to see me, as though I have dropped in unexpectedly without an appointment. He shows me around. Some rooms are closed off. I wonder if he lives here. Next door is the Wright bicycle shop. He gives me details of their lives as though he knew the boys. Then he tells me that he was stationed in Norfolk during the war flying B52s. He hasn't been back to England since. He brings me a coffee. He says he's a retired school administrator.

I want to tell him what I have experienced at the State Pen. As I left the prison, with Lindi Holman's apologies and solicitude, her small face convincingly concerned, I began to shake and had to stop the car. I was shaking with hatred. Yes, bring back the death penalty, bring back disembowelment. But I can't tell him. I listen as he talks about England as he remembers it: the Fens, the landgirls harvesting; the boat rides on the Broads with a girl called Doreen, whom he should have married, the bombers coming back over the North Sea, not always at full strength, the huge horses being used on the farms — 'just like the ones we got over there on the Firestone Farm' — and then a pub which was called The Fox & Grapes.

'I love that. That's so British. The Fox & Grapes. Don't ever lose that, that kinda gentleness. As I get older, I'm seventy-five, I often think about England.'

I could tell him what kind of country it has become: I'm an expert, but what's the point?

Gloria will be waiting to hear my story. She will be busying herself with the Christmas decorations and the Steuben glass and the lights (there are voltage problems) and all the other trims, but she'll be thinking about my meeting and any messages I can carry to her. I can't tell her that a dreadfully deranged psychopath began to masturbate looking at Belinda's picture, inflamed by the sweet, dopey graduation smile.

'You all right, sir?' asked the guide.

'I'm fine. I enjoyed talking to you. Any charge for the coffee?'

'That's my personal coffee, there's no charge. Your people were wonderful to me during the war. Where are you headed, we close in half an hour?'

'I want to see the Menlo Park Laboratory and the Cotswold Forge.'

'"Laboratory". I like the way you say that. I remember that. "Labo-ra-tory". You better hurry. That's quite a hike.'

I leave him in the snug, wallpapered cottage. The old sit-up-and-beg bicycle outside the shop is being put away. I enter the laboratory, where Edison first made an electric light glow, and see Gloria vividly. There is nobody else there except for a guide who glances at her watch, as if fearing she is going to have to do her spiel for me. And in the glass factory — a lot of glass was needed for the lightbulbs — I see exactly where Gloria and I hid away. Nothing has changed. We stood there; and I felt her heavy — too sumptuous — breasts right there.

Now I head out back through a white-painted picket gate. I can see the sails of the Cape Cod Windmill and near that, if I remember right, is the Cotswold Forge. I walk briskly, almost jog.

Everyone is a god who has the freedom to create his own truth.

Everyone, even serial killers, can take refuge in claptrap.

Despite the frost in the air, an oily, grey Detroit frost, I smell the reek of nullity in his mineral breath. I can imagine his truth. I feel a compulsion to accept Belinda as my own now. How dare he call her a cumslut? The word itself is disgusting: it even sounds mechanical. But then what had I — what had Gloria — expected of a man who has murdered at least six women?

What did I think, that it would be a picnic?

I cross the wooden bridge to the windmill, the planks yielding under my feet. I can't see the Cotswold Forge. For a moment I think that maybe I've forgotten it all, or misunderstood or falsified. But then I see that some trees have grown up, sheltering the forge from view. I round them, and there it is: a drystone wall topped with snow, the low-hanging roof shading, like heavy eyelids, the windows which glow yellow. I enter the house, stooping slightly. The walls breathe the honeyed warmth of youth and innocence, so utterly different from the prison.

Here in this inglenook, where they have a log fire glowing, my fingers found their way into Gloria's pants and further into her sweet pussy. Why pretend? It's an incomparable feeling, one of the high points of youth, a finger sliding into that willing and yet mysterious place. Yes, these are the stones quarried in Middle England, these are the huge smooth flags. Even the horse brasses, hung beside the fire, pub trinkets, reassure me. I sit now in front of the dying fire in an elm ladderback chair. I am inside Henry Ford's Arcadia, and I understand absolutely why he chose to spend so much of his later life here, patrolling the village green, visiting the smithy and the print shop, just a few miles from his plant, the greatest industrial plant the world had ever seen, one which is slicking the River Rouge with yellow and strident green and turning the skies red and gaseous. And I see that Gary Pale Eagle has done the same thing. And I see too that in my way I have constructed my own flimsy refuge.

Everyone is a god who has the freedom to create his own truth.

In the Cotswold Forge, before the glowing fire, I sit suffering from shock. I know I'm in shock – the cold, the trembling, the difficulty breathing – and at the same time I feel that I have peered into something unspeakable. And worse, something which will leave a stain on me. I remember reading that hope was a phenomenon of human life. I remember reading that hope was the medicine of the miserable. Scott Hollinger, to whom I went as a messenger to bring back hope to the Christmas tree gal, has killed hope. I've never given hope much thought, until now. All those people, hoping.

Gloria hopes that I can bring her some comfort. Why has she drawn me into this? Why did I allow myself to go and see this madman?

The fire is warm, but the scents of the wood ash there are unfamiliar, resinous and pinous. An elderly woman tells me that they're closing in five minutes. She too looks like a retired person, retired from the turbulence beyond the perimeter wall.

It's a long walk back, past George Washington Carver's Cabin and the lake where the paddle-steamer plies in summer. The lake is frozen solid, but its shape is clearly drawn, absolutely flat in the undulating landscape. There are other houses – Greek revival, slave cabins, Gothic – in the trees. All of them are here to represent some expression of hope. Hollinger was a no-hoper from his early schooldays. And I see now that being a no-hoper is a crime against America.

Gloria, I spoke briefly to Scott Hollinger. He didn't say much, just that he regretted deeply the fact that he was driven by inner voices – the classic symptoms of schizophrenia – to commit his murders. This is his message, which he particularly wanted you to hear: If he had had the drugs earlier, he believes he would never have done it. But he wanted you to know as Belinda's mother that she did not suffer. She barely had time to know what had happened. He begs your forgiveness. He will never be able to forgive himself, but takes some comfort from the fact that he now knows that he is a paranoid schizophrenic, who should have been treated many years ago. He hopes that, with the passage of time, you will get over your loss. For himself, although he knows it would be no comfort to you, he has found salvation in God's love. He will never be released, but for his remaining years he will try to live according to the Holy Gospel.

Cumslut. That is what he said.

Henry Ford's village is still as I reach the main gate. But I see two giant horses being led away to a red barn against the toxic sky.

11

I have taken a keen if unscientific interest in the brain. I have read many articles by researchers, but none seems able to answer the question of how the brain is both a complex computer and the location of our selves. I once snatched a conversation with a small, famous professor at a cocktail party. The brain, he said, was essentially an organ developed in the course of evolution to make meaning out of what comes flooding in. (I think I have it more or less right.) His researches suggested that the brain did this routinely, not waiting for us to order it into action. Before I could get on to the interesting question of how the conscious 'us' might command the brain, we were interrupted by our hostess carrying a bowl of delicately blotched quail's eggs. She was shiny with sociability. The brain seems to make meaning. But I believe it also tries to protect the lodger, the self. (Or is the brain lodging with the self?)

Stephanie accused me many times of avoiding things which disturb my carefully composed world. Privately I did not regard this charge as particularly damning. After all, who wants to disturb his tranquillity? In the last few months of our relationship, she would call me at the agency, even when I was in meetings and say: 'We have to talk.' What she meant was, she had to talk and

I was obliged to listen. In the guise of openness, a sermon was concealed.

After my encounter with Scott Hollinger I see just how I have tried to protect myself from the world. Certain things are unknowable and incomprehensible. It would be far better for Gloria to have accepted that her daughter – our daughter – was murdered by a man whose mental wiring was seriously faulty, a computational failure, than to try to make contact with his self. The pathway leading from our lovemaking in Thomas Jefferson's bed to this philosophic blunder, is tortuous. I think the trouble arises from the belief that there is a remedy for every ill, an answer for every problem. Except one. Gary Pale Eagle has solved that one: he refuses to recognise a distinction between death and life; they're part of one continuum, just scenes in a never-ending play.

I pull in to call Gloria, and I lie to her. I am trying to close off this dangerous line of thought which could lead to more shocks.

'Gloria, I think you should let it rest now.'

'Thank you for what you've done. I really do appreciate it, Dan.'

'There comes a time, I believe, when you must let go.'

'I am trying to live day by day.'

Our conversation is underscored by the Christmas music.

'I knew, Gloria, when I spoke with Hollinger, that Belinda was our child,' I say suddenly.

Gloria seizes this.

'Did he say she looked like you?'

'Yes. When he looked at the photograph, yes. But there was more to it.'

'What, then?'

'It was a feeling, let's say a strong feeling.'

'You didn't believe me before?'

'No. It's not that. This is just an acceptance.'

'You opened yourself to your deeper self.'

'I am not ...'

'I gotta go, there's five people wanting to discuss trims. Oh shoot, only four now. Bye. Love ya. I'll come by when I'm done.'

She sounds girlishly happy, elated. I am, if anything, more drained than I was as I left the prison. I cannot bring myself to go out to the car. Instead I take another coffee, standing in line amongst some very fat people. They are frolicsome, not at all concerned as they rumble and puff and heel towards the cash desk with mountains of cookies and giant racks of ribs, the animal's torso clearly rising from the plate, struggling from the grasp of the heavy sweet caramel-coloured sauce that has been ladled over it.

My coffee has become mysteriously cold and watery. I am paying now for having thought that serial killing is a colourful item of Americana, like Graceland or Jim Swaggart or the World Series. I am making some recompense. I see that Gloria wanted to cast me as the lost parent, come home and reconciled, and I accept the part.

Cumslut.

I take out the picture and stare at it. She looks nothing like me.

'Refill, honey?'

'Oh, yes, please.'
'She's beautiful.'
'It's my daughter.'
'She's real cute. And intelligent, obviously.'

The waitress smiles, her face cracking in long pleasant fissures. Waitresses have a history: they've been around the track and seen things, particularly the curiously restless nature of men alone, and I turn my face up to her to receive some human understanding.

'She passed away.'
'I'm so sorry. That's awful.'

But I've gone too far. She doesn't need this. Nor do I. I feel guilty: I drink my coffee and pay quickly. The waitress avoids my glance. She detects something unsound.

Now I'm driving again up the highway – north is up – up the highway, into the night.

12

Gary has been away for a couple of days. He doesn't say where or on what business. He has to go to the mental hospital for stabilisation from time to time, so perhaps that's the answer. He is silent as we drive, his head locked downwards, so that when I glance at him I see an Easter Island profile. I want to talk to him about Gloria, and Scott Hollinger, but he has lost me. He begins to moan quietly, but it is not a distressing noise. Perhaps he is speaking to the Great Spirit. Gary told me that the Great Spirit said to the Prophet that he did not make the Americans: 'They are not my children. They are the children of the Evil Spirit.' The Great Spirit backed the wrong team when he sided with the English in 1813, but I didn't say this.

Gary is wearing a pair of jeans, a buckskin jacket decorated with porcupine quills, and his elaborate necklace. On his head he wears a black, battered hat, with a high crown. On his lap he holds his otter medicine bag. Its scent, smoky and animal, is perfuming the car.

There's been a partial thaw so that now the countryside is wet. In places the snow has melted completely, revealing plants and grasses and the remains of cornfields, tired and lifeless. A car passes with a deer trussed and spreadeagled on the bonnet. When we come to a junction in the road, I look questioningly at Gary and he gestures to tell me the way. He cannot speak.

His brown eyes glance up at the trees, which are shedding snow like rooftiles falling, only briefly. He gives the appearance not of knowing the way so much as sensing it. When he holds up his huge hand to indicate the direction, it is like the blade of a paddle. We pass now between two small lakes, icebound except in half moons near the road, where sheets of ice are floating free in the sunlight and a few unseasonal geese are paddling nervously. A sign reads *Bay Hills Reservation, Welcome*. We pass a handicraft store, shuttered for the winter. Outside are some carvings of thunderbirds. Now I see trailers in the woods beside the road. Each trailer has a comet trail of lame or completely derelict cars and pick-ups, and some also have rusting fridges and worn-out settees lying around. Gary gestures for me to turn off down a track.

After a few miles he says, 'Stop here.'

We walk a little way from the car to what looks like a playground of some sort bounded by a picket fence which is in need of repair.

'Burial ground,' he says, forming the words with difficulty.

I follow him through the gate. Set among trees in the melting snow are what look like small dog kennels.

'Spirit houses.'

The words are uttered slowly and painfully. He kneels in the wet snow and I do the same. I have come to see that there is a lot I will never understand: the other night at Willi's Sausage Haus, Karen said, 'You gotta go with the flow,' to explain her relationship with Duane.

Gary takes some objects from the bag, an eagle feather and a strip of skin, and lays them beside the grave. Then he begins to chant. I recognise the call to the spirits.

Man e do, we ha, pe-me so win. Wa ka-ka no, ho shi-a de.

He sprinkles some tobacco on the snow. It is pungent in the still, cold air.

Ka wi ka da an na we wa si na.

Gary's voice is freed now from whatever was holding it. It has risen to a high, resonant pitch, emerging from his nose. He chants the chorus.

He-he-he-he-he – *yo,* and I join in, although my knees are wet and chilled.

We are teetering on the edge of farce.

After a while Gary packs his bag and we rise, stiff in the legs. He smiles at me.

'They send you greetings.'

Whoever they are, I am pleased to receive their good wishes. We drive off into the woods past trailers, and a wooden crudely carpentered Baptist church. Down a partly overgrown lane we stop outside a trailer which has a huge panel hanging loose revealing some yellow-green insulation material. Smoke is rising from the rusted and patched chimney. Children's vehicles, broken and discoloured, are emerging from the snow. Gary leads the way. We enter the trailer. It is dark in there after the bright sunshine and snow outside. Sitting at a table is a man of about sixty. His dark hair is tied back, in what I take to be Indian style. He wears a working man's checked shirt, buttoned up to the neck. In his hands he holds a mug of coffee. A television is on in another part of the trailer. He and Gary speak briefly in what must be Ojibwa.

'Dan, I want you to meet John Rattling Hawk. John, meet Dan Silas,' he says with curious formality.

We shake hands. His hand is oily as though he has been handling fish.

'How are you?' he asks, listlessly.

His face is the colour of nicotine, and strangely swollen. His belly, on a slight frame, is large and tumorous. His eyes are pouched and lidded. We sit at the table. A silent, elderly woman with grey straight hair, also tied back, brings us coffee. She is wearing a stonewashed denim jacket over a long print skirt. She returns to the television, and I can see her motionless silhouette against some once-jaunty blinds.

Gary and Rattling Hawk speak for a while. Rattling Hawk fetches a pipe, the bowl carved to represent the head of a bear, and they smoke in turn. I take one puff when offered. The smoke is harsh, causing me to cough. Rattling Hawk smiles briefly and wanly, and says something to Gary. They smoke slowly and deliberately; then they sing some words, *Ki to no bi in, ne he he*, which are designed to put them in touch with the spirits. The spirits respond to this sort of chanting, a wake-up call, so that wherever they are roaming in whatever realm (I haven't figured out the eschatology) their attention may be engaged. Nothing can proceed without their approval. They are always ready to be consulted by those who know how. I can imagine that this is very comforting.

When I arrived back from the penitentiary, Gloria was in my room asleep. I was dog tired myself, the tiredness that strong – overwhelming – emotion produces. I longed to sleep and to forget about Scott Hollinger and my rashness. But I had to wake Gloria and tell her comforting lies. I watched her, reluctant to get to the business in hand.

As she lay there, her face half turned upwards, like a swimmer taking some air in the middle of the crawl, I was struck by the fact that it is impossible to know anyone else. You can never begin to know what is going on inside them, although, like the geysers of Rotarua and Yellowstone, you get intimations of the forces below. We have been made to be inscrutable. Even our altruistic acts are self-serving. Perhaps only identical twins have an inkling of what it is like to understand another person.

Gloria released a small sigh and a snuffle. When we were seventeen I imagined I knew something about her. But even her virginity was an illusion. Her face was slightly fevered in sleep and, without the focal points of her beautiful eyes, seemed blank and pointless.

Only in limited areas you can achieve profound understanding. Sex is one of them. Stephanie and I had revelled in delightful, excitable excess, involving cars, staircases and an object she called 'plastique Bertrand' after a French pop star, a one-hit wonder, but this shared delirium was also to become an obstacle: it left both of us weakened, our moral immune systems open to reproach. In my foolishness, I had seen our adventure in Jefferson's bed as having some shared significance for Gloria and me, a bond of understanding. I should have known better.

Eventually I woke Gloria by holding her hand and squeezing it gently.

'I'm sorry, I'm sorry. I was so tired,' she said, confused.

'Don't worry.'

'I tried to stay awake.'

'I was late. I had to stop off because of the roads.'

I couldn't mention Greenfield Village.

167

'I will just freshen up. Don't look.'

She went through to the bathroom, and I glanced briefly at her legs, her bra across her soft back and the meridian of her pantyhose bisecting her rear, which was reasonably broad, but just about right for a Bavarian of her age. I heard the noise of water and the lavatory flushing. These intimacies I found appealing.

'Okay,' she said, 'start at the beginning.'

She was wearing the Bavarian skirt now, which was crumpled, but she looked fresh and excited. I described to her the prison and the procedure.

'And then I was shown into the visiting room. He was already there, a sad little man, I thought, completely zonked on drugs now, repentant as I said on the phone, really nothing much there.'

But I was going too quickly. I had to describe my own frame of mind, and the exact conversation word by imagined word.

'I felt at peace when he said he was sure she hadn't suffered.'

I was trying to take up some of Gloria's burden.

'And you felt sure she was your daughter?'

'Absolutely.'

'Fred ordered blood tests when we divorced. She wasn't his daughter.'

Oh Jesus, how can I put this thing to rest, I wondered. Next she's going to ask me to produce a blood sample. But she didn't, instead she kissed me and left. It was two in the morning. I tried to sleep but lying next to me, breathing on me, was the appalling *untermensch*, Scott Hollinger.

Gary Pale Eagle and his chum John Rattling Hawk are standing.

'Can you follow, please?'

They're a strange couple, Gary with his head fixed downwards and his hat tilting forwards as a result, tall and unmistakably Northern European, and the much smaller, hunched unhealthy Indian figure of John Rattling Hawk, unmistakably a son of the forest.

I follow them through the wet snow and the derelict toys and deeper into the woods. We come to a giant metal container, the sort of thing you see being loaded on to ships, and John Rattling Hawk takes his keyring, attached by a thin chain to his belt, and unlocks the padlock. The bolts are stiff; the pair of them have some difficulty releasing the catches and sliding them back. Rattling Hawk strikes a match on the metal and lights a lamp. As it begins to push back the darkness, I see that the whole container is lined with shelves, and the shelves hold all sorts of objects.

'These are our crown jewels,' says Gary. 'They are the things we have recovered or preserved along with many skeletons. All the skeletons have been returned, of course.'

'This is mostly Gary's work,' says Rattling Hawk. His voice is curiously flat.

'This material is available for our people ...'

They take me on a brief tour of the artefacts: snowshoes, bows and arrows, lances, carved thunderbirds and bears and owls, sacred posts, coloured in bands of green and red, wampum belts and necklaces and lacrosse sticks and headdresses and body ornaments and calumets in all shapes, and hundreds of drums and medicine bags and canoes and pots and baskets.

'Dan, I have told Johnny that you will try to recover for us some of our things from the British Museum. Some of these things we have recovered from the Smithsonian and the Cranbrooke and many universities, but what I want to show you is unique and irreplaceable.'

Johnny Rattling Hawk takes me to a tall metal closet, locked and bolted. Gary smiles at me encouragingly. In the tall hat, with his conspiratorial smile still lingering on his long face, I am reminded of a scene from Oliver Twist: 'Dodger, take off the sausages; and draw a tub near the fire for Oliver.'

The closet opens. On one level are what appear to be rolls of cardboard, stacked neatly. Beneath are some tall posts.

'These are the few remaining birchbark scrolls and memory posts of our people. They recall our travels and migration, they recall great hunters, they are the notes and music of our songs. Some people, like Johnny, can recite many mide songs, our sacred songs, with the help of these charts.'

'Gary also can recite the mide.'

'What we have here is a pitiful collection of our artefacts. Some individual mide priests still hold charts passed down to them, but many have been destroyed and many are held in museums.'

Gary has lost all his hesitancy. He sounds like the boy who used to lead our debating team, eager, his words tumbling just behind his bright thoughts. I find this glimpse of him moving.

'The pictures on the scrolls are mnemonics. The work of one person is not fully intelligible to another. When you were attending Oxford you probably took lecture notes. These are like lecture notes. What is missing is the scroll or scrolls which give us a kind of master plan. But we believe at least one of them is in the British Museum. These are the war songs. They never changed. We know some of the words and some of the pictograms, but we need to find the key, otherwise much of this is useless.'

He reaches up and takes down a scroll.

'It is birchbark. This one is probably one hundred and twenty years old. It's the record of a hunting song, belonging to a priest. Look, here are some elk and here's the camp, the hunting camp with tipis. Most times our people lived in lodges. And here is a beaver, indicating a beaver hunting ground. Priests would give these to hunting parties to guide them to the prey. They knew from fasting and trances where to find them.'

The birchbark is incised with very rudimentary figures, animals, trees, tents and outlined people.

'Now, these in the store are the ones we need to be able to translate. They're the few surviving scrolls of our ancestors who travelled from the great oceans. If we can understand them we will be able to know a great deal about our history.'

'A lot,' says Rattling Hawk. 'Yes, a lot of history.'

'We know from our researches what these scrolls look like. They are seven feet long and about eighteen inches wide, stitched together with birchbark twine. There may be one or more in the British Museum.'

'Are the scrolls on display in a case?'

'No, no, they don't know what to do with them. They don't know what they have. They're kept for scholars in a storeroom. It's in London. Do you know a place called Hackney?'

'Yes, I know Hackney. I know where it is, at least.'

'My information is that you can apply to view artefacts. Someone like you, an Oxford man, will have no trouble.'

'And then, what do you propose?'

It's very cold in the container. Gary considers my question seriously for a moment.

'I propose that you make a substitution. We have a few scrolls, not good quality or very interesting, that you can use to make the switch.'

'You make a switch,' says John Rattling Hawk, gravely.

'Have you applied for them to be returned?' I ask. 'Would you like me to ask if that is possible?'

'Dan,' says Gary. 'Dan, one thing I've learnt is that if you tell a museum or a Government agency that you want something real bad, they discover that they want it even worse.'

We stand in the gloom, surrounded by these things made of bark and hide and wood.

'Have you stolen many objects?'

'We don't see it as stolen. That would not be our point of view.'

'Definitely not,' adds Rattling Hawk. 'Not stealing.'

'I'll think about it,' I say.

'I dreamed that you would come back when the time was right,' says Gary.

I follow them back to the trailer, where the woman has prepared some wild rice for us, served with stringy pieces of meat. Gary is silent again, and eats carefully, his huge hands delicately picking through the food, his head clamped downwards.

Before she left the hotel last night Gloria told me that I had aroused in her strong feelings that she could only describe, she said, as 'detrimental to her life'. A terrible charge and similar to things Stephanie has said: that I wanted love and admiration, that I wanted people to think they had some special understanding with me, but that I was not prepared to give in proportion. Gloria had seen me sauntering down the steps of Alexander's on the King's Road with my miniskirted and velvet-jacketed chums, and she had fled. Gary Pale Eagle had gone mad and become an Indian, and I had never once enquired after them. The worst of it is that apparently for all these years they have thought about me continually. But I have apparently been detrimental to Gloria's life, and possibly Gary's too, in ways I can't imagine. With Stephanie it was clear that I had not loved her as she wished, that I had – in her telling anyway – used her. I am troubled now by the thought that I may have been responsible for more unhappiness than I knew by arousing expectations I couldn't fulfil. I wonder how this can have come about, and if there is an unconscious will in me to cause unhappiness. If so, I am in urgent need of the enlightenment the migis promises.

'The bears were once a part of our tribe, but they returned to the woods,' says Gary, unexpectedly, when he has finished chewing.

He and Rattling Hawk talk in low voices. I can eat no more of the wild rice which tastes nutty and clings to the roof of my mouth. Rattling Hawk stands up and goes outside where the sun is sluicing the countryside with a pale evening rinse.

'Rattling Hawk wants to give you a gift. Have you something to give him in return?'

All I have is a small silver keyring from Liberty's with a polished stone something like an opal set in it. It was given to me by my secretary at the agency when the Japanese showed me the door. I begin to unhook the keys. The keys remind me of my white house, of course, but they also tell me that I am far from home.

Rattling Hawk returns, stamping his feet, with a small cowrie shell on a leather thong. He gives this to me without comment. I give him the keyring which he glances at briefly before putting it in the capacious pocket of his rough shirt. Gary is silent on the long drive south, silent that is if we're talking about conversation, but inside his head — inside his self — things are happening. Music or chants or long-lost conversations are being played. His head nods, his face closes up and opens again as readily as a sea urchin, and his eyes gaze upwards and then he smiles. His hands suddenly plunge sideways like Jerry Lee Lewis playing the piano; and he issues a range of noises, short bits of song or sighs or Ojibwa phrases; much of it sweet and strange. He is as mad as a hatter, but whatever he is in thrall to has an enviable nobility.

'Dan,' he says suddenly, 'our people never kill a deer when it is swimming.'

I'm not sure where he is wandering but wherever it is, I wish him godspeed.

13

Fred Larssen has the look of a man who has recovered from a serious road accident: he stands up from the table and walks stiffly to greet me, his huge shoulders still appearing to have football pads squaring them off.

His girlfriend, Jeanne Lamoureaux – a 'Cannuck from Montreal' – has left him. It's a temporary separation while she finds her own space, but it has been going on for a coupla, three months now. To tell the truth he can't see her coming back. Fred's got a job selling Hallmark cards – the black folk around Gary love cards – and he coaches a little football too. All in all things are somewhere between medium okay and shit. He shows very little interest in my past – why should he? – but he asks me if I always spoke this way. I explain that we were always English, only kids pick up accents fast.

'So you want to know about Gloria, I would guess?' he says amiably, after our drinks have been served.

We're sitting in a small bar, very dark although it's mid afternoon and he should still be out on the road. His huge frame was shaped for football, by some unknown agency. But now it looks to me like the River Rouge plant, built for a purpose long obsolete. Just as the plant is rusting and crumbling, so Fred's hugeness and squareness are rickety. His surplus muscle capacity is useless. But he retains traces of the jock's confidence in his manner.

'First off, Dan, you know that I was screwing Gloria since her sophomore year. You came along when I was away at Lansing, but I would still see her. Gloria and Karen and I and her fella, who also was on a football scholarship, would double-date; hell, they were up for most anything. The point is she kinda began to look over her life when we were breaking up, after I met Jeanne. If you ask me, she decided maybe you would have been a better bet. Easy to say afterwards. She spoke about getting in touch with you again.'

He orders another drink. The first one has gone down into the large frame like a spring vanishing underground in the mountains. His nose is damaged. Not by football, but by life, by disappointment. It has always been a puzzle to me why the nose should register human failings.

'I was never a bet, Fred, I was just a high school romance.'

I want to encourage this downgrading after Fred's revelations, which have hit me harder than I would have imagined after all these years.

'She saw something in the fact that you and she had – she says – done it in old George Washington's bed. I never believed that, by the way.'

'No.'

'Although she said you shot your wad in about ten seconds. Anyways, when Belinda died, she asked me to take a blood test. She wanted to prove that I was not the father. Jeanne told me to tell her to take a flying fuck, but I just stalled. I was never much for math, but the mathematical probability that you was her father after one dingdong in Mount Vernon ...'

'Monticello.'

'Monticello or wherever — same difference — when we had been doing it for three years, the mathematical probability seemed to me kinda off the chart. Are you ready for another?'

He summons a waitress, who is wearing a short shiny skirt. She carries a small but distinct belly, which is straining the red material of the skirt. Three men enter, cautious at first, but quickly expanding in the gloom, like those dried mushrooms you soak in water, filling out. They are soon demanding twists and crushed ice and splashes of this and that.

'Belinda was my daughter. She looked like me; people used to say so all the time. Even when she was knee-high to a grasshopper. She went a little strange in college, drugs and so on, but she was a great kid.'

It's true they look alike. In the photograph Belinda has the same deep, slightly too wide-apart eyes.

'Gloria said you didn't go to the trial.'

'I didn't. To be honest, I wasn't sure if I woulda been able to control myself. This Hollinger guy was a sicko, but it seems he had been seeing her for about two weeks before he killed her, and I somehow didn't want to hear any details of their relationship. I didn't want anything to spoil my picture of Belinda and also, seeing as I'm trying to give it to you straight, I didn't want to hear that she had psychological problems because of me. I didn't want to show up in court and sit there with Gloria glaring at me, like blaming me.'

Fred is giving it to me straight. With his slightly slurred voice — this has come on fast — and old-fashioned slang, he's delivering one blow after another, without meaning to.

'What do you mean, Hollinger had been seeing her?'

'They were dating. Hollinger was a drifter, but he was kinda believable apparently. He said he was a paramedic, some bullshit story about being sent all over the country because of his special skills, and she believed him. Dan, in my experience women believe all kinds of garbage if they want to.'

There is no doubt who he's referring to.

'Anyways, after the trial, that's, what, two years ago nearly, Gloria began to see all kinds of weirdos. At one point she was talking to some 5,000-year-old warrior through a medium, that's what Gene told me, and also she was talking to Gary Beaner who's been in and out of the state mental institution. I mean, you know it goes on and on. Beaner became an Indian chief or something – can you believe it?'

'What was she doing with Gary Beaner?'

'Gene says he is a traditional healer now, using Indian medicines. He helped her a lot, so Gene says. He told her Belinda was happy in the spirit world. What the heck, if that makes her happy, I'll buy it.'

As he drinks deeply from his third whiskey sour, I wonder if he has anything more in store for me, but no, the well is dry. We talk about the old school and lost opportunities. Like many athletes, his life peaked early. The people who remember him running in three touchdowns against Iowa State are few. I see that past prowess can become a burden, as with movie stars who were great beauties, always remembered for a certain scene at a certain moment in their lives. In the gloom of this South Bend, Indiana, bar with the conviviality rising as the working day ends, I am struck by the strange, lonely phenomenon of individual lives. All these people trying to assess and marshal their lives, relying on feelings for evidence, metaphors for reality and myth for guidance.

All these people, all America, under a compulsion to justify to themselves or to anyone who will listen. Mr Zabruder, who loved Emerson, used to quote: *Each philosopher, each bard and each actor has only done for me as if by a delegate, what one day I can do for myself.* Emerson has a lot to answer for. It's the realisation that they are not perfectible which weighs on all these Emersonians. America is a country of disappointed individualists.

Fred says he should have taken the job in the public relations department of GM but instead he tried to play pro ball. His cruciate ligament went. By the time he came out of hospital, the job had gone to some stuffed shirt, and he started coaching full-time at Hollybush. Belinda was three, and he had to earn some money. Gloria was disappointed.

'Did she ever mention the possibility that you were not the father at that time?'

'No. Never. Look, like I say, that all came after I started seeing the little Cannuck.'

His great wrecked face, red and plumped up, is on the brink of collapse. God knows what it will look like after the fall. There's a certain fascinating tragedy in Fred, as he sculls steadily down the river and out of sight, with no idea of how to stop himself.

Our conversation has staggered to an end. Without protest, Fred lets me pick up the check and we emerge into the raw, unforgiving street, just at the point where the suburbs begin to collapse into the broken-backed city. It's a zone where you can buy drugs and drug-dazed prostitutes. Some young white boys are cruising, looking for trouble — beefy boys piled into a big old car. I remember our excitable forays into Flint.

Fred and I shake hands. His car, he says, is around the corner.

'Look, Dan, anything more you need, you know where to find me. All you got to do is call.'

All you got to do is call. He walks showily as if he's ready to jog over to tight end, calling attention to his useless size, an athlete's walk, lumbering, strutting, down towards the thrift store and the car lot. These strips are all the same, a sort of busy evolutionary seashore.

It's a long drive from Indiana. But car journeys are a natural state of affairs: the country is huge; it demands motion from its restless citizens. I am happy to lose myself in this vastness. I will never see Fred Larssen again. Why do I care? Because we are bound together, although he doesn't see it that way, by our interest in Belinda. And I am party to Scott Hollinger's dreadful cruelty, something I wanted to discuss with Fred but couldn't. Fred seems to have drifted off into a half-lit world. But he, unconsciously, has not spared me either. I wonder why Gloria never told me that Hollinger and Belinda had dated. I had simply assumed that he had seized her off the street or at the school or something. And I wonder why Gloria told me that Fred had demanded a blood test. And most of all I wonder what Gary Pale Eagle told her about me.

Indiana. Indian country. On a thong around my neck I am wearing my cowrie shell, the migis, which Gary said was a token of enlightenment. So now I have my bear claws to make me invisible and my migis to give me wisdom. I can't see much on either side of the highway, but if it is true that the spirits inhabit every object in space, they are well camouflaged in this Indiana landscape, which may bear their name but seems to have lost all trace of them. The Indians have moved from the actual to the mythological landscape. I will return with the birchbark scroll, if I can, to help them navigate to where they belong. I see a turn-off to Tippecanoe, before I hit the highway north along Lake Michigan. Tippecanoe was the scene of a battle with the Shawnee Prophet, which General Harrison used as his election slogan when he ran for the presidency: *Tippecanoe and Tyler too.*

When I arrive back at the hotel it is nearly three in the morning. There are messages for me. Gloria wants to know where I am. And my lawyer in London tells me that Stephanie and Krupat are cutting up rough. He wants to talk. It's mid morning in London. Lawyers are always in meetings and may never answer their own phones. There is some baton-passing before I can speak to him.

'What time of day is it with you?' he asks.

'It's three a.m.,' I say.

'Out on the razzle dazzle?'

He is full of a particular sort of English self-regard, which sounds to me affected at this distance.

'Not exactly. What's going on?'

'Your former partner took umbrage at something you said to him. He is prepared to come clean with the tax authorities and Companies House and send them a cheque, with interest, unless you pay Stephanie. His story is that you and he — particularly you — made a mistake buying some property which should have been declared in the accounts when you sold, and he has now taken advice ...'

'Pay her.'

'Everything?'

'Not everything everything, but make a reasonable settlement. Half the shares.'

'I thought you said we'd given her enough.'

'We have, but that's not the point.'

'Do you want to sleep on it?'

'No.'

'Are you pissed?'

'No, I'm not pissed. I've just driven from South Bend, Indiana.'

'I get my kicks on Route 66,' he warbles.

'For a lawyer you're quite tuneful.'

'Thanks.'

'But you've got no idea of geography. Pay her today.'

'I'll need that in writing.'

'We'll make an agreement today. I'll sign it when I come back.'

'And when's that?'

'Soon. I've got some business to settle.'

'Have you gone native?'

'John, find out something about the British Museum Department of Ethnography, can you?'

'It'll cost you £200 an hour.'

'Good night, John.'

Carefully I lay the cowrie shell beside the bed, and then run the bath, wondering if the Niagara rushing of the taps, which is underscored by roaring pipes, will wake the people next door. I bath and then I pay to watch a movie called *Hollywood Casting Couch*. In this movie young women – slightly foxed young women – come to a casting suite and are soon enjoying all sorts of sexual activity on a desk and a couch. The story is a familiar one: there are girls from small towns, eager to become stars. I turn it off, and lie in the gloom. I have agreed to give Stephanie, even in the lower range of her demands, a sum of money which will mean that I have to sell the house within a year or find another job.

I can be a bard, a philosopher, an actor.

The thought cheers me and I compose myself for sleep. It's a state, sometimes lasting only a few seconds, when the day's events and thoughts throw in the towel.

It's strangely welcome as though sleep is not so much to rest the body as to provide a respite from being human.

14

I wake early to the phone. It is Gloria, asking me where I have
been. She says we had agreed to meet yesterday for lunch at
the old drugstore in Hollybush. I can't tell her that I have been
to see Fred. It would be a betrayal of the confidences, however
incomplete, that she has entrusted to me. But I still have some
questions. Why did she give me Belinda's photgraph if she knew
Hollinger was, as Fred put it, going with her? And why has she
not told me that Gary gave her Indian medicines and interceded
with the spirits on her behalf? But I don't ask her the questions.
Nor do I tell her what Fred said about blood tests. Instead I
apologise, saying I have been out in the boondocks with Gary
on some crazy mission. We agree to meet after work.

'I'm not on the late shift tonight. Some things are more
important than work, don't you agree?'

'Absolutely.'

'Gotta love ya and leave ya, the old folks are becoming restless.
Any minute now they are going to torch the place if I don't get
out there.'

Monticello. The sun is hazy but extremely hot. Jefferson's trees
are wilting. A bus pulls up in the carpark beneath the house. A
boy – lean, full of turbulent ideas and urges – walks up to the

house next to a girl with heavy breasts and a sweet smile. Her hair is long and straight. She has been screwing a college football star, for three years, a fact which she has kept from the eager boy next to her. This lad imagines his detailed and protracted exploration of her body as something of an idyll, a sort of poetry. It is about to come to a triumphant conclusion. He feels it. All the same, he is keenly aware that first sexual experiences are poignant because they are unrepeatable. They indicate a terrible fact, that you can never drop anchor on the ocean of time, not for a single day.

I see this boy so clearly, waiting in the last group of the day on the generous steps beneath the front door to be admitted, shaded by a tree Jefferson himself had planted. The southern humidity is causing Mrs Anstruther to fan herself with a guidebook. Mr Zabruder is moistly eager to imbibe a fresh draft of the civil religion.

Now the boy is returning to the bus, as the sun is going down behind the Blue Ridge Mountains off to the west, and the heavy Virginian air exhales the rich scents of dogwood and magnolia and the medicinal vapours of the locust bean. These scents are congratulating him.

He walks with Gloria, holding her hand, but he sees this as a mainly personal achievement, indicating a certain panache, and marking the end of his high school career appropriately. But of course, on a less exalted level, the love and adoration of the second-most beautiful girl in the school is important.

On the bus back to DC, Gloria apparently sobbed, but now it appears that I was the one with the grievance.

I believe I am taking pleasure in seeing things differently, in being wised up to the fragility of my assumptions. I think maybe my life is like one of those old masters which reveal something more interesting underneath when they are cleaned or x-rayed. Perhaps my deception by Gloria was a perfectly natural thing: she loved me so couldn't bear to tell me of her previous sexual shenanigans. Strange though, that no word of it reached me.

I order my breakfast. The hotel life, the placelessness, is growing on me.

At Monticello I was intrigued by the idea that Jefferson had built tunnels under the house so that the slaves could scurry about unseen, fetching and carrying, tending to the carriage horses, while Jefferson and his Virginian cronies talked states' rights and animal husbandry. But I didn't know then that Jefferson was probably fathering children by a slave, Sally Hemings, in the very bed where Gloria and I made love. It adds some retrospective poignancy to our story, I think, and possibly some connection to Emerson's universe.

When we went back to England, my view of English history was formed entirely by my knowledge of American history. I was amazed to find that Britain had been a great power. And it surprised me at first that the English did not take the Founding Fathers and the Constitution more seriously. Not all Europeans, I came to realise, believed that the clear principles of Jefferson and company were a major breakthrough for a monkish world. Now it looks as though many Americans believe the Founding Fathers were running a racket, a cover for other activities, such as property accumulation and the exploitation of women.

Gary's mother calls. Gary wants to speak to me urgently. He has been taken into hospital again. I ask her why.

'Gary has beliefs which are not always acceptable to the local people. He chants his songs in public. Things like that. So he has to go and be medicated for a while. It happens quite regularly. It's a pay-off.'

What does she mean? Briskly she gives me the address in Grand Rapids.

'He wants to see you urgently. Don't worry, it's a private place, all very civilised. Goodbye.'

So I am on the road again. Unlike Fred, who is on the road to sell, I seem to be buying. I have driven further in the last few days than I travel in a year in London.

I have never been in a mental hospital. Of course I am familiar with them from movies and even from the accounts of friends. Mental hospitals seem to suffer from an error of logic, namely that all the victims of disparate forms of delusion or depression can benefit by being confined together. Also, there is obviously an element of punishment, punishment for being disturbing. Drugs are used in place of handcuffs and bodybelts and straitjackets. They are places where the human spirit has been known to flourish gloriously and defiantly, but I suspect it doesn't happen very often. A friend of mine described his Chistmas in a mental hospital after a deep fit of depression: one of the psychiatrists came with his three cringing children to sing carols with the inmates on Christmas Eve. My friend stood there in his dressing gown singing 'Hark the Herald Angels Sing', watching the wretched children forced to hold hands with the patients. It was a turning point on his road to recovery as he realised that the psychiatrist was much crazier than he was.

The countryside has been beaten into submission. Yet a pale sun, a timid watercolour, is softly breathing life on the woods and fields and farmhouses. *I became a transparent eyeball*, said Emerson. How Mr Zabruder loved that phrase. *Nature always warms the color of the spirit.* It's easy to understand that the vast wilderness encouraged thoughts of the sublime. I see from my meetings with Gary and Rattling Hawk, that the Indians were only able to express themselves by means of natural objects. What a calamity to discover that the whole universe of trees and lakes and deer and useful plants was nothing more than a backdrop for the white man's restless activities. What a calamity to discover that the unchanging – the laughing waters, the towering sequoia, the silent valleys – could change. It must have been a kind of excommunication. No wonder Gary Pale Eagle wants his scrolls back and his ancestors safely buried, never mind the fact that he is no more an Indian than I am. In his mind he wants what is logical, the restoration of certainty. But I see that in the many years I have been absent, this has become a popular refrain around here.

And now I pass a lake, Lake Odessa, and in the floating contact-lens sheets of ice and the water glistening feebly in the newly hatched sun, I see Gary Beaner floundering, as he did in Harvard Yard, trying to swim among the autumn leaves. There is no point in it: the spider's web can never be put back together by hand. None the less, I must help him, even as he drowns.

Asylums, nut-houses, always have gates. This one has a large pair in wrought-iron. Their severity is mitigated by a sign reading, *Grand Rapids Clinic, Welcome*. On the driveway up to the house, a Victorian mansion, two men are striding purposefully. I look at them closely to see if this purpose is illusory, but I can't tell. They ignore me.

Gary has a small tidy room in a wing to one side. The furniture is unmistakably institutional, rounded edges on the table and chairs and bars on the windows made to look like louvres. He is sitting in one of the curved Scandinavian chairs of blond wood with an orange backing. The deliberate cheerfulness of the fabric is depressing.

'Gary, how are you?'

'Oh, you know.'

He is wearing a bathrobe in a washed-out saffron colour, like a Buddhist priest's, and for some reason he has on working boots. His head appears to be clamped very tightly, so that his chin cannot leave his chest.

'Do you need anything?' I ask.

'Aw no. They know me pretty well here. This is my room.'

The drugs have silenced his little noises and stifled his inner writhings. I miss them. I watch his long, bony face. Only his eyes under the opulent lashes are moving. That's all they've left to him. They roll in agony and for a moment I can see nothing but the whites, which look like newly peeled boiled eggs. My heart, which appears to be becoming more mercurial every day, cries out. Inside my chest I can hear it screeching, although muted by ribcage and other human tissue.

I kneel beside him and hold his hand.

'Take your time, old buddy. When you're ready.'

Old buddy.

'Dan.'

He stops. The gears have locked.

'Dan, I can't talk to the spirits here, because of the drugs.'

'Yes. I'm sure.'

But he says no more. I wait for a while and then get off my knees and release his giant hand. A young nurse, in a trim pastel-pink uniform, comes in with coffee. She hands Gary a mug, and pats his shoulder affectionately, and smiles at me. I sit on the edge of his bed waiting.

There is a tremendous struggle going on, expressed only by the wild eye movements.

'Dan, if you go to my home, you will find the birchbark to take to London to make the switch. My mother has it for you. I have also left some papers for you to read.'

These words come out in a rush, like a stammerer's sudden damburst.

'I'll get it.'

After a few minutes, he speaks again.

'Dan, when Gloria was so troubled after Belinda died, I spoke to the spirits.'

Now the words are coming more freely. It seems as if he has difficulty connecting with what he wants to say, as if the neural pathways are too numerous and too overgrown for him to find. But once he has started in the right direction, the way becomes clear.

'I spoke to the manitous. They told me that Belinda was your daughter and I told Gloria. It seems she had believed it for many years. And then I gathered medicines for her in the woods, white sumac and the root of the snakevine, which I gave to her to see more clearly, and I suggested that we should ask you to come back for the reunion. And she gave Gene your address.'

'That's fine.'

So I have been fingered by the manitous.

'Dan, to make your peace with Belinda, you must go to her grave and speak to her. Go with Gloria. A child in the shadow world must speak to her parents, to be happy.'

'How do I speak to her, Gary?'

'Do you remember the song?'

He stands up with difficulty, and begins to chant, his feet shuffling on the clean, clean, clean floor:

Ka wi ka da an na we was si nan.

I follow, mumbling the words – if they are words – with him.

The young nurse passes, but mad behaviour does not detain her.

He-he-he-he – yo.

We chant the chorus, three times.

After a few minutes he sits, silent and rigid. My eyes are filled with tears as I look at him.

'Are you all right, Gary?'

But he is mute now. I leave the room to find the nurse.

'He most likely wants to go to bed,' she says cheerfully. 'He's a real sweetheart. We'll look after your friend, Mr Silas. He often speaks about you. He said you were coming. Your first name is Dan, right?'

She touches my arm as she says this. I walk along the pastel corridors; in one room I see a woman sitting on a bed nodding urgently, like an oil rig. The only noises are of urgent vacuum cleaners and distant, rushing, sluicing water. Perhaps hydrotherapy plays a big part in treatment.

He often speaks about you.

What was there to speak of, that is the question? I was a regular sort of boy, perhaps a little too sure of my own worth, but still an incomplete creature, nobody you would want to invest much of your human capital in. Yet I am deeply touched. Perhaps his old life, as a clever, grave, oddly assembled Midwestern boy, ended at Harvard and I remained trapped in his memory like that hunter found in a glacier in the Dolomites or wherever it was. And maybe he continues to feel our boyish closeness undiminished. For all those years he has experienced the ecstasy of youthful friendship without realising just how quickly it passes.

The area around the clinic has some huge houses. One looks like a Frank Lloyd Wright; another is built in the style of a French château, and another reminds me of the Cape Cod house and windmill, all weatherbeaten shingles. I stop at the lights outside a timbered Tudor mansion, now the Davenport College of Business. Visits can be made by appointment to see the Tiffany ceiling and the murals by Gilbert White, the son of the lumber baron who built the place.

Gary's mother is listening to public radio, something to do with the debates between Clinton and Dole. Her eyes are feverish; I think her face is too intense for someone of her age. There should be a release from an interest in politics.

'Some debate that's going to be. Oh boy. A PR event, more likely,' she says. 'How is my son?'

'He seems good, all things considered. Maybe a bit quiet.'

'They drug him to the eyeballs. But I guess they have to do it. Have you come for a package?'

'Yes, I have.'

'It's here. It's some of his Indian stuff.'

'Yes, it's for a museum in Britain. I'm taking it.'

'You leaving us again?'

'I'm going back for a while anyway.'

'There are some papers too.'

She gives me a fat, battered, brown envelope.

'He thinks you are still seventeen, you know.'

'I was wondering about that.'

'Well, I must go,' she says, 'I don't want to miss anything. Goodbye.'

The sunshine has failed. There is a baleful look to the late sky. Some children pass by, staring out of the back of a station wagon moodily.

If I am to speak to Belinda, what will I say to her?

As I drive, with my birchbark scroll and the dog-eared nonsense safely stored in the trunk, I ask myself what has happened to me. Why am I allowing myself to contemplate praying to the Great Spirit to put me in touch with Belinda, who looked so like Fred Larssen, a drunk selling greeting cards over in Indiana? And why have I conceded to Stephanie and Krupat, once my friend and close associate, now both so hurt and angry? I am struggling for an answer, but I know that it can be found in the albumen of Gary's eyes and the obscene jingling of Hollinger's manacles and the thought of Gloria standing forlornly in the King's Road.

Now I see the windmill, *De Zwaan*, which Gene told me was the biggest authentic Dutch mill outside the Netherlands. The sky behind it is full of fury. The huge sails are beating gracefully, just like the wings of a swan, grinding flour to be sold in gift packs.

15

Gloria has arranged to take some time off work. We're going to go down to the cemetery together and in the evening meet some people. Gene and his wife, Karen and Duane are coming to Detroit to say goodbye. My flight is booked out of Detroit and it's there at a seafood restaurant called Captain Nemo on the river that we're going to take our leave. Gloria tells me that she and I once drove down there in her car and I bought her dinner. Up to that point it was the most sophisticated and glamorous thing either of us had ever done. She said that we ate soft-shell crabs and bluefish. I don't remember the occasion, but the restaurant at least exists. I know this, because I have made the reservation.

I'm waiting for her in the drugstore. I hope she is not coming in her Bavarian outfit. My coffee and a bran muffin are served by the Chinese girl with small, dark pupils, like the pips in an apple. It is quiet. In this lull I feel the old village, which was a place of deep stillness. The activities at the high school, then across the road, the marching band practising and the football coach shouting and the Glee Club harmonising, would give way to a prolonged, tree-lined quiet, which as a boy I found disturbing. Afternoons were interminable. I longed then, and Gary and I discussed it often, to get away to places where we believed this oppressive stillness would be avoided. Now the Chinese girl chats to a boy near the cappuccino machine, which is hissing quietly. This conversation, I think, is forced on them by boredom.

'Hi.'

I start. Gloria is standing there beside me in her overcoat holding a small bunch of flowers.

'I snuck up on you. What were you thinking?'

'Oh, I don't know. Just about the old school. How quiet it was in the afternoon.'

'You were far away.' (She draws out the 'far'.)

'I'll have a latte, Serena, skimmed milk,' she says to the waitress, who is glad to break away.

'Okay, Mrs Larssen. Comin' up.'

Gloria takes off her coat and goes to hang it on a coatstand. When she heads back towards me I see that she is wearing a white blouse with a dark waistcoat and a grey textured skirt. She looks like the wife of a college professor, or as I imagine one would look.

'You look wonderful,' I say.

'I feel so happy. And it's all thanks to you.'

She sits opposite me, and squeezes my hand.

'How's that?' I ask.

'Because you've helped me put this thing to rest.'

We sit for a moment in an eddy of silence.

'Dan, was it Gary's idea to go to the cemetery?'

'Gary has a way of anticipating what you're thinking, don't you find?'

'He told you about Belinda?'

'He only said that you and he had discussed the whole thing.'

There are small lines around her eyes, what look to me like impertinent graffiti.

'You are right about him. He does seem to know which way your thoughts are going. How is he?'

'He's in the clinic at the moment, but apparently this happens from time to time.'

'Yeah. He gets kinda wound up, tight like a spring and they take him in for a coupla weeks and bring him down. It's like a cyclical thing with him.'

'Has he ever talked to you about his Indian, his Native American life?'

'He was arrested once with some activists. They were opposing the building of a road over a burial site. Also he knows a lot about traditional medicines, which, by the way, I believe in one hundred per cent. He gave me some and they helped me a lot.'

'How often do you see him?'

'Why are you giving me the old third degree, Dan?'

'No, no, it's not the third degree, it's not that at all. I just find him fascinating.'

'You and he were always close.'

'Gloria, that was twenty-seven years ago.'

'Twenty-eight, but hey, who's counting?'

The coffee arrives. I'm a little irked for a while. My life has been full of incident: I have met well-known people, including Salvador Dali (mad, but shrewd) and Prince Charles (shorter than you would imagine), many exciting women (including an actress who almost received the Oscar), yet here in Hollybush my whole life is seen to be defined by the high school senior trip of 1968, by this almost plump, smiling woman and what we did in Thomas Jefferson's bed. Even today's pilgrimage springs directly from that moment, real or imagined. Now I think I've stayed too long. It seems like months, but actually it's only a few days.

'Was it Gary who told you that Belinda was my child?'

'Gary helped me along the way.'

'Gloria, Gary is crazy. The question is, why would you believe a crazy person if he told you something which he couldn't possibly know?'

'I knew. I already knew. And Gary knew. I believe that you must only accept that which is true to your inner self.'

'Would that be something like believing that every person is a god who has the freedom to make his own truth?'

'Kinda, but it's more a question of inner listening. You don't just go out there and make your own truth. You find what is true by tuning in. It's not in books or what your parents told you. Unfortunately. I wish it was.'

Something's gone now. The air has thinned. I want to hasten to the cemetery and get on with it. I smell Hollinger's dead breath. But Gloria wants to talk about us. We are now tied together, we are *us*. If Gloria and Hollinger both believe in the unmediated relationship between the individual, however mad, and the truth, where does that leave us? Maybe as Fred suggested, there is the reek of complicity in this business.

'Gloria, I have to ask you this: is it true that Belinda and Hollinger were friends, were going out together?'

'That's a terrible thing to say. That's what he said at the trial. Where did you hear that?'

'I looked at old copies of the *Journal* in the library.'

'That was just about the worst thing he said. He tried to

make it seem like nothing more than some kind of lovers' tiff. Can you believe it?'

The Chinese girl brings the check.

'Those flowers are so beautiful,' she says.

She glances at me briefly, expecting that I will say something to elucidate the relationship between the beaming, snappily dressed Gloria, the flowers and myself. But in truth, I would find that hard to do. I feel myself on very shaky ground, preparing as I am to talk to someone in the spirit world.

'Have a nice day, now.'

'Dan, Belinda was not going with Hollinger. Not never.'

'They said he was a conman who went around befriending women.'

'He met her at some college kids' bar, just casually. There's a big difference. He tried to use that in his defence. And that's what he said about all the other girls too. Jesus, Dan, put it out of your mind.'

'Okay.'

I can't.

Belinda is buried in the cemetery of Benton, not in Hollybush, because it was in Hollybush cemetery that Hollinger was detained, trying to bury the almost dead woman in a fresh grave. Who was going to notice the disturbance? Except that many people now take their cues from television, and this ruse has apparently been well used by television scriptwriters, so Officer O'Keefe told me. I feel, as we drive the few miles to Benton, that there are too many reminders of made-for-TV movies in this whole business which tug at my spirit. We leave Hollybush by way of the lake, past a factory outlet store, selling brand names. The world is gripped by a mania for brand names.

'I'm ready to start my life again,' says Gloria. She rests her hand on my thigh. 'Are my hands cold?' she asks.

'No. Can't feel a thing.'

But I can. I feel a writhing, snaking current, which comes from way back when we used to park by the lake, to watch the submarines, as Mr Zabruder called it. I think now that he took a lively sexual interest in his class, when we arrived bruised around the mouth and etiolated in the morning.

'Do you remember when you were punched by a boy from Benton who was trying to set our homecoming bonfire off?'

'Yes.'

'You whacked him. I was so proud of you.'

I can't remember the incident.

'Dan, what's your status in your personal life? I never asked. We had so much catching up to do?'

Catching up, but only in a very limited area.

'Oh, I am living on my own now. My girlfriend Stephanie and I split up a few months ago.'

'Do you miss her?'

'No. Well, that's not entirely true. I'm getting over having her around.'

What I would like to tell her is that while I am happy without Stephanie, sometimes even ecstatic as I swim in my own, undisturbed thoughts, I also wonder if I couldn't have married her as she wanted and been acceptably happy, at the same time making her happy. But the feeling that I could never shake off was that she had changed the rules. Now Krupat is getting me back for not supporting him: I ratted, not just on Stephanie, but on him.

'That doesn't sound a trillion per cent convincing,' says Gloria.

'Probably not. It's complicated.'

'Ain't it just,' she says, widening the subject. 'When we were kids, making out here by the lake, life seemed simple.'

'True,' I say, but even then I didn't believe it.

'You don't imagine how many questions life is going to throw at you,' she says. 'Do you remember where we used to make out?'

'Not exactly, not the place.'

But I remember many small inconsequential details.

The snow is lying quite thick and wet in the cemetery. Cemeteries out here still retain their origins as fields, just on the edge of the towns. There are simple headstones and a few small flags stuck in the snow. An AIDS ribbon decorates one slab. It is clear which graves have been visited recently by the pathways made by feet. In Jerusalem I once walked on the Mount of Olives and saw the small stones the living leave on the tombstones. It seemed to me a wonderfully honest memorial, that the piles of stones on the older graves were scattered or absent, just like the people who had left them.

Gloria leads me to the graveside. The slab of granite (even at this moment I wonder if it is a composite material) reads:

Belinda Larssen, 1969–1994.
Sleep with the angels.

'That's beautiful,' I say. 'And simple.'

'Now I truly believe she is sleeping with the angels.'

Gloria places her flowers in the snow, and bows her head. Her lips are moving. I close my eyes and chant.

Ka wi ka da an na we was si nan.

I chant the words silently, once, then again and attempt to imagine the spirits listening to me, which I find an attractive idea. Although I try to conjure Belinda from wherever she is in some form – any form she chooses – I fail.

I mouth the chorus, *He-he-he-he – yo* a number of times, and I strive to capture exactly the intonation which my mad friend has taught me. All I can see is Belinda in her graduation photograph, the faint smile of achievement, the rolled-up certificate with its ribbon and her Larssen features.

But as Gary has asked me to, I leave a message in the air in case as a result of my chanting she can pick these things up. I assure her that I will always remember her. I also wish her godspeed wherever she is. I am not sure if in the spirit world you are voyaging from one region to another, or if those distinctions are forgotten. At the same time I am also concerned about the confused ecumenical signals I may be sending.

Gloria kneels and says the Lord's Prayer out loud. How poetic it is. For the second time in a few days I find myself kneeling in the snow. It makes me think not of the spirit world, which I take to be light and airy, but of the dark earth beneath the snow, cold and dense.

We walk from the cemetery hand in hand; Gloria smiles at me although her eyes are moist.

'I am so happy,' she says.

'Me too.'

'Can we go to the lake for a while?'

So we drive back towards Hollybush, and turn down a snowy

lane on the far side of the lake, past the farmhouse where Gary's family used to rent out the barn for dances, and then through to what in the summer must be a landing stage and slipway. There are some small craft under wraps, lined up abandoned to the winter snow which has almost buried them. We park facing the lake which is now mostly frozen over.

'Do you want to kiss me?'

'Yes.'

I kiss her. Her tongue outlines my lips.

'Butterfly kiss,' she laughs. 'Remember?'

'I remember.'

She tastes pleasantly of coffee still. She leans against me, she holds on to me, and my face subsides into her hair, which is stiff with lacquer, and scented lightly of roses, I think. The lake is restless, as though the ice is subject to many conflicting forces in these interim days before the freeze has finally set. We sit silent for a while, tightly embraced.

'Shall we go?'

'Let's go, Dan. Are you glad we came here?'

'Yes.'

And it's true. She kisses me lightly. I hug her once more. The windows of the car are beginning to mist over, so there is a little fiddling with the controls before we set off.

16

Because of Duane we are going via Tiger Stadium. He tells me the names of the greats who have played here: Ty Cobb, Charles Gehringer, Micky Cochrane, Reggie Jackson and Lou Gehrig. And many more. Nobody else wanted to make the detour to Corktown, because that part of Detroit is blitzed and menacing. Karen believes we will all be mugged. But anyway we drive down there, Gloria and me and Duane in my hire car, and Gene, his wife and Karen in his Cadillac. Gene's wife is about thirty. She has second-wife looks, slightly ill at ease, but also keen to show that she can fit in and be a sport. She told me she had been to London. Gene had an arm around her shoulders when he introduced us, as if she, being younger, was in need of extra protection. She is pretty, but it is not going to last, because she is somehow featureless. A standard Midwestern look, which subsides fast into anonymity. Her name is Gayle. She takes care to explain the spelling because it lends her some distinction.

Before we left the Holiday Inn, Gene said he heard I had been kinda active. He smiled suggestively.

'You've been getting around.'

'Loose ends,' I said lamely.

'Loose ends. What's that supposed to mean?'

I wonder if he has spoken to Fred Larssen.

'Nothing special. Gary wanted to see me so I drove up to Grand Rapids.'

'How's he?'

'He's pretty silent.'

'Yuh. I'm afraid that happens. What did he want to talk about? Gloria?'

'No. As a matter of fact, I wanted to talk about Gloria, but he wanted to tell me about Ojibwa memory scrolls.'

'And you went to see Hollinger. I called you back, but you had gone. How did that work out?'

'He just fed me the line. He said he was sorry, he is a schizo, he should have been on medication earlier.'

'And you believed him?'

'It was mechanical, absolutely meaningless. He's past caring. But he could have said anything, I mean what's he got to lose?'

'That's true. Dan, are you planning to come back?'

'I don't know.'

'You must come back. Take your time, but come back when you're good and ready. Gayle likes you, by the way. I can tell.'

Gene wants to gather in all his sheep. I wonder if I will come back here ever.

As we approach Detroit, Duane is increasingly eager to talk baseball.

'Mike Illitch owns the Redwings and the Little Caesar pizza chain. He is the owner of owners. This guy is a marketing genius. Kids can run around the bases Mondays. From Memorial Day to Labor Day he sets off a bunch of fireworks every Friday. Dan, this is the last of the old ballparks.'

Duane is sure that I would know about Lou Gehrig's last game at Tiger Stadium. Lou Gehrig must have given his name to the disease. I ask Duane.

'That's the one. Muscle-wasting disease, all-time tragedy. This is where Reggie Jackson hit a homer on to the upper deck roof in 1971. It's a small ballpark, but that was one hell of a hit. Do you want to stop?'

'No, thanks,' says Gloria.

Behind, the Cadillac is idling nervously. The stadium rises from the surrounding devastation like the solitary building in the ruins of Nagasaki.

'Ah shit, okay, let's go, but you better believe me, this is the finest ballpark in the country from the fans' point of view, not that anybody gives a fuck about the fans. Take a last look. There ain't gonna be another, that's for damn sure.'

We drive on through the ruined city. Now we are passing an immense complex on the river with two huge towers peering through the dense air towards Canada.

'Renaissance Center,' says Gloria.

'Some fucking renaissance,' says Duane, who is sulking.

'There's an awesome panorama from the Steak House on the seventy-something floor,' says Gloria.

I wonder if she has been there. We leave the city, hugging the river. Nobody remembers exactly where the restaurant is, but eventually we turn off past the sign for Belle Isle. The streets here were once lined with pleasant wooden and brick houses with porches. Now there are more gaps than houses, and those that are standing appear to be derelict. The side roads leading off are littered with bricks and rocks, lying in the brown slush.

'Are you sure this is right?' asks Duane.

'Yes. It's the right road, it's got to be here somewhere.'

207

'How long since you was here?' asks Duane pointedly.

'Duane, just because nobody gives a fuck about your baseball, you don't have to get mean with me.'

'Oh, I'm so sorry. I really am. Am I, shit.'

At that moment we see a spotlit sign, *Captain Nemo's Famous Seafood*. We enter a razor-wire compound beside the restaurant, guarded by two large black men, whose clothes curve outwards to accommodate their huge blimp shapes. They take the cars and point us to the restaurant.

'Jesus, I'm so hungry I could eat the crutch outta a low-flying duck,' says Duane.

Karen is reunited with him, but wary.

'Duane, for Chrissakes, this is a special occasion,' she says.

'Whaddid I say? All I said was I'm starving, that's all.'

Gene puts his arm around Gayle and smiles, as if to tell her this is no big deal, nothing more than a little horseplay. Gayle smiles too, but with ominous restraint.

Inside the restaurant there is life and warmth and bustle. Fish restaurants provide a special air for us to breathe – marine, nourishing and primal. A television is on over the bar, showing ice hockey, and a small circle of men is watching that. Duane stops to watch, but Karen takes him by the elbow. Further down the bar we have cocktails. Gloria sits very close to me, her knees pressing against mine. We study the menus. We are up a level from the river, which contributes to the marine atmosphere.

'They don't have soft-shell crabs,' says Gloria, her knees insistent.

I see that this is some sort of anniversary for her, not just my farewell. I order sea scallops and bluefin tuna and a bottle of Napa Valley champagne. Our table is by the window looking out across the water to Canada. Outside on the river a ship passes, moving surprisingly fast. For a moment I catch sight of a man on the bridge, looking intently, but competently, ahead, and then he's gone.

'Two kindsa clam chowder. I'll take the New England one,' says Gene. 'That's where they invented it, right?'

The waiter is watching the hockey, holding his order pad, which is a small computer. 'I believe that's true, sir.'

Gloria is going for the Maryland crab cakes and shrimps creole.

'Maryland is a long ways away, I'll take a steak,' says Duane. 'The surf and turf without the surf.'

Karen sighs: 'This is a fish restaurant.'

'No kidding. I was wondering what all those marlin and nets was doing on the wall.'

'Oh Jesus, Duane, Dan's going away and you're making a scene.'

'I'm making a scene? Hello. I don't think so. You know what's wrong with this country? We've turned into a nation of piss-ants. We're not allowed to say what we think. *Fish is so-oh-oo good for you. Steak is for rednecks. Oh please don't smoke because of my po-fucking-tential allergies.* You gotta pretend all the time. You gotta pretend you like jiggaboos. Jesus, nobody means it, but they're all so fucking scared to say so. We're all scared. We're scared of what, we don't even know what.'

Gloria says, 'You don't look too scared to me, Duane.'

'I'm scared of one or two things. Like death for example.'

'Lighten up, Duane,' says Karen. 'I think we just had such a great time as kids. It was a blessing, but only now we see there's a downside to being so happy. We never thought. I don't know, we were just in and out of each other's homes like family.'

'And each other's panties.'

'Fuck off Duane, we were in and out of each other's homes and Hollybush was our little world. We didn't want any more, we didn't know any more. I mean I can remember every sidewalk and every blade of grass and every damn house in the whole place. Upstairs and down. Something changed.'

'We grew up,' says Gene. 'For me, looking back, the change came when they bombed Michigan, Ann Arbor and set the draft board on fire. I couldn't understand it. It was for no reason. It was just like we had it too good, there must be something wrong, you know what I'm saying?'

'Hollybush was a place, a real place,' says Karen. 'Now it's a dormitory. We don't know half the people in the condo. They creep in and out. They're from someplace else.'

'Now look who's becoming depressing,' says Duane. 'Dan's leaving, remember.'

'Are you coming back Dan, like you said? You gonna buy a summer place?'

'He's not coming back. Not now he's met us again,' says Duane.

I can actually see myself as we sit there. I am distinguished not by my appearance, but by a watermark. I have seen Scott Hollinger, and he has stained me. I wanted to kill him. It's a shocking feeling, but also exhilarating.

'I'll take stock when I get home,' I say.

Gloria hasn't asked me about Hollinger again. She's sure the well is capped, but I think I can smell gas escaping.

'You know, I think the thing we didn't appreciate is that

you have to grow from your experiences,' says Gloria, her eyes reflecting the light from the candle which rests in a red bowl on our table.

'Oh Jesus,' says Duane, but too quietly for Gloria to hear.

'No, I mean what we didn't see then was that our lives have a meaning and a purpose which you must look for. It's not going to come – kaboom – straight at you. You have to find it. I certainly didn't realise that until recently.'

And of course we nod respectfully, because we know to what she is referring. The obvious lesson of life is the one the cheerleaders don't want to contemplate, that life has no sense to it. For some people, but not for me, this is a difficult thing to accept.

'I mean there's different ways of looking at this. I don't believe we have to over-analyse it in psychological terms,' says Gene. 'What has happened in our country and to us is just the play of forces. We should welcome it and accept it.'

'Gene, you should run for the legislature,' says Gayle sharply. 'That's Clinton baloney. We don't know what the fuck to do so let's pretend to be happy.'

We are surprised that Gayle should enter this arena, our arena, where the words don't mean what they say.

'There speaks a young person,' says Gene proudly. 'I love you, peanut, because you stop me turning into my dad.'

'Too late,' says Gloria, and we laugh.

The food arrives on huge platters, decorated with submarines. We're all twenty thousand leagues under the philosophical sea here, I think.

'To absent friends,' I say, raising my glass. Gene wants to drink a toast too.

211

'Here's to our class, and to our friend Dan. I hope that now he's found us, he will return many times.'

'That's beautiful, Gene,' says Gloria. She turns to me. Her eyes are wonderfully deep. 'I hope you will, Dan. And thanks for the toast.'

She's talking about Belinda, I realise. I cannot now sever this tie, which is a rope plaited together from strands of sentiment and lying.

'Oh God, this is so fun,' says Karen. 'Thank you, Dan.'

Another ship comes by, with a giant ice-breaking prow, pushing the black, dense water roughly aside.

In my heart I am voyaging down the river too. I am wearing my bear claws and flying into the upper regions with the thunderbirds. They speak to me, but I can't entirely make out what it is they are trying to tell me. Eventually I alight and go to see my old friend sitting in his pastel small room, and I invite him to come with me. He stands stiffly.

'Yes, thank you Dan,' says Gloria.

'To absent friends,' I say once more, to Gloria and Gene and Duane and Karen and Gayle, and Gary Pale Eagle.

17

Near the canal in Hackney two boys of about seventeen are crossing the road. They are thin, quite small. They have earrings in both ears. They wear Nike caps and bulky jackets. Their legs poke down straight as sticks. They are walking fast, diagonally across the road.

'She's fucking lezzer, that's what it is.'

'I don't fink so, she's 'aving a baby.'

'Anyone can 'ave a baby.'

They're gone, down the steps to the canal. I cross the canal by a stained brick bridge, generously arched to allow horses pulling barges to pass under it. The sky hanging over Hackney is featureless; the clouds must be there but they are a morose grey colour, the colour of a blanket in a sanatorium. Drops of rain are falling, but it's not certain that they have fallen from way up there; they simply seem to be cavorting in the air, like mayflies. Down below on the towpath the two boys are standing now, lighting cigarettes.

I am carrying two wallpaper bags from Colefax & Fowler. In one I have the scroll, in another a roll of Bailey Rose wallpaper. My request to view certain artefacts has been granted. The building is down a dead end, just across from the bridge. My request states that I wish to view various items which I have identified from the catalogue at the British Museum's Department of Ethnography. These include a wampum belt (Chippewa), a birchbark canoe (Ottawa), some ceremonial drums (Saskatchewan) and some birchbark scrolls (Great Lakes; origin uncertain) and a collection of calumets, peace pipes (various origins). They are all shown and numbered in a catalogue at the Museum of Mankind off Piccadilly, but are stored here in Hackney. At the reception desk an elderly man in uniform stands. He finds my name in the appointments book and directs me upstairs to reception.

'We had a Zulu witchdoctor 'ere yesterday,' he says.

'What did he want?'

'He was only looking for 'is grandfather's skull, wasn't he?'

'Did he find it?'

'No. He never. His name was Credo.'

'Anywhere I can find a toilet?'

'Yes, sir, just upstairs, outside the lift before the reception.'

I deposit the scroll in the toilet, high above the cistern, which is of the very old-fashioned sort with a chain, prized by decorators. The tiles in the urinal have a greenish glaze, but that may be a chemical event. At the reception a middle-aged woman with short bleached hair signs me in and asks to check my bag.

'That's nice. Do you mind me asking how much it was a roll?'

'Thirty-two pounds.'

'Thirty-two? Bloody hell.'

'It's a very small room. It's a loo.'

'That's lucky. I'll call someone to take you to a viewing room.'

Soon an elderly man in a brown coat arrives. He coughs twice before he speaks. All Cockneys are unhealthy.

'This way, please, sir.'

The whole place is bronchial, the heating pipes wheezing, floors hacking, windows phlegm-stained.

'We're moving next year. This is all going to be closed down. All high tech and computers and whatnot. Yours truly won't be moving to the new premises. Not required on voyage.'

In a long room, looking on to a well of blind windows and seeping bricks, is a big table, covered by a dust sheet. The porter removes the dust sheet.

'These are what you ordered, I hope, some of 'em. Most of 'em haven't been off the shelves in thirty years.'

I can see the scrolls immediately, but I take my time. I start by examining the child's cradle. It is decorated with electric patterns of beads and shells and rests on wooden runners. From the handle, no doubt for pushing it in the snow, hang some small, bronze bells. I make notes and attempt a sketch. The porter sits on a chair reading a paper.

'How long have I got?'

'Take your time, sir. We close for lunch, but you can come back.'

The sled has a handwritten note attached to it which reads: *Acquired by Lt. Amberly Alleyne, 1812, Fort Dearborn, Michigan.*

Lt Alleyne also collected the wampum belt. But it is not the King's Great Broadaxe. The belt, like my bearskin necklace which I am wearing somewhat uncomfortably under my shirt, has spiritual value. I see that Indians were unable to distinguish clearly between the natural and the symbolic; they didn't want to, as a matter of fact. As instructed by Gary, I sprinkled some of his powder on the doorstep as I left the house.

The wampum belt, as I write painstakingly in my notebook,

215

is made of bark string, sections of quills from a porcupine, and small shells. The quills form a pattern on the string in the shape of a line of tipis, although I can't be sure this is the intention. At one end it has two tassels, decorated with larger and smaller shells one after another. The twine from the birchbark is soft. I ask to borrow a ruler. The porter leaves the room for a few minutes.

At lunchtime I take my Colefax & Fowler bag and change it for the one hidden above the cistern. I walk down the canal towpath for half a mile or so, past the warehouses with smashed windows, past a lock and a basin full of stubby boats tied up. There's a pub here, and I sit at a window looking out towards the City. These unimpressionable areas, still with a foot in the last century, are the eastern approaches to the City's temples of marble and granite, which are so necessary to accord money its proper respect. At the time of the sale, Krupat and I had a few meetings here. The bankers were pally with money, and this closeness had left a dusting on them, like the pollen from perfect, expensive, lilies.

I called Gloria once at the Christmas Wonderland, and she wanted to know why I had talked to Fred Larssen without telling her. Although the Christmas music behind her was cheerful, there was a deliberate flatness in her voice, which reached straight inside me.

'I didn't want to tell you, because I just had some questions for Fred.'

'Like was I nuts, for example?'

'No, Gloria. I didn't want to usurp his fatherhood, without seeing where he stood.'

There was a pause and I heard sleighbells and carols playing.
'Is that a fancy way of saying, you didn't believe me?'
'No.'
'I gotta go. Christmas is a-comin'.' She said this coldly.
'I'll call you.'
'If you want. I'm not going anywhere.'

I can picture her now in her Bavarian skirt and generous white blouse among all the Christmas baubles. I wonder if I have some quality which causes anger in women. Or perhaps something fatal has worked its way into the relationship between men and women, something that has been caused by the promotion of the self. The self is entitled to satisfaction in all spheres. Women – certainly the sort of the women I have knocked about with – can see no theoretical limits to their fulfilment, so they conclude that the limits they actually bump into – sexual, financial, romantic et cetera, are the result of male hegemony. And, in theory, I would find it hard to disagree.

I also called Gary Pale Eagle. A kind voice at the clinic told me that he was definitely calmer. I could leave a message, but he couldn't come to the phone right now.
'Tell him I'm on the trail.'
'On the trail?'
'Yes. He'll know what that means.'
'Okay. If you say so.'
She's used to speaking to the deluded.

When I return from lunch I say hello to the woman at the desk. For a moment I fear she's going to look inside my bag again.

'Not been out buying more wallpaper, have you?'

'No, just eating a sandwich.'

'I'll call Les. Hang on a mo.'

The porter arrives; his lungs are not functioning as they should, because the walk back to the viewing room leaves him short of breath. I work my way slowly through the exhibits. The calumets, the peace pipes, were also collected by Lt Alleyne in the region of Fort Detroit, 1812. They come in the shape of a bear, an eagle and the head of a bison. They still smell faintly of tobacco, I think, although perhaps I am making an association with Gary Pale Eagle's aromatic lodge. I take my time before moving on to the birchbark scrolls. The first is labelled: *Ojibway music scroll. The scroll of Chief Bad Boy. The various animals denote notes of music.* The scroll is neatly incised and I start to make a record of the tipis, arrows, beavers and whitefish which are depicted.

'Do you want a cup of tea?'

'Yes, please.'

'How do you take it?'

'Dash of milk, no sugar.'

The porter sets off down the wide, clanging corridor. The second, bigger scroll has pictures of encampments and tipis and what look like ladders, just as Gary has described it to me. I quickly make the switch. The substitute scroll is smaller, and the bark is noticeably lighter in colour. As I replace the label, I read on the back: *Collected by Lt. Alleyne, Battle of Thames, 1813. (Tecumseh relics) Tecumseh, the Shawnee Prophet.*

Les, the porter, arrives with the tea. I feel my breathing constricted; he and I are both having to search for air.

'How's it going?' he asks.

'Not too bad. Nearly finished. Where does this stuff come from?'

'These things? Quite a lot of it is in Storeroom C. It's called the Alleyne Collection. Most of it's rubbish. Nobody's really logged it or nothing like that.'

'Can I see the storeroom?'

'Are you finished here?'

'Yes.'

'Members of the public aren't supposed to go down there. But what's the point. It's all going. Let me just lock here first.'

And he leads me down a back lift. The lift is one of those with a concertina door which starts and stops with a terrific jolt. We enter a huge vaulted storeroom. On wooden, slatted shelves, leading off into the gloomy distance are thousands of vases and drums and assegais and bows and arrows and knobkerries and musical instruments and masks and figures carved of wood and stone and coral. From the roof hangs a collection of canoes, kayaks, makoros, dug-outs and snowshoes.

Les leads me to the back of the room and into a large alcove, like a wine cellar, lined with shelves. A card written in copperplate reads: *Alleyne bequest. Collected by Gen. Alleyne in North America and Africa between 1798–1836.* There are no details about Alleyne.

'Can I have a look through this lot?'

'Go ahead. Be my guest.'

It is clear that young Lt Alleyne collected avidly. He was at Fort Dearborn, the site of Tecumseh's most famous victory, famous particularly because he spared American captives. Alleyne appears to have collected souvenirs, anything from letters to General Harrison to tomahawks. Some of these are neatly labelled, others have lost their provenances. Les tells me he has to close soon. I am rifling through the objects fast now. There are waterbottles

219

and fragments of scrolls and ceremonial rattles. Then I find on a crumbling burlap bag this note: *Medicine bag. Gen. Tecumseh killed at the Battle of Thames, October 1813*. I can't be sure that I will ever be allowed down here again. While Les is closing some windows I stuff it into my trousers and close my jacket. When Les returns, I press twenty pounds into his hand.

'Can I come down here tomorrow?'

'Certainly, mate. Why not.'

I notice that he's not calling me 'sir'. Bribery diminishes the giver more than the taker.

Outside the store it is dark and wet. The streets of Hackney, where Tecumseh's sacred medicine bag came to rest, are weeping from the bricks, like plaster saints in Spain.

So now I have two precious relics lying on the floor of my living room, which Stephanie took to calling the drawing room. I have borrowed a book on Tecumseh, and I have looked in the *Dictionary of National Biography* to find out what I can about Alleyne. When General Procter was reluctant to fight, Tecumseh, who had been commissioned as a Brigadier General, threw off his scarlet tunic and took up his medicine bag and painted his face and adorned himself with eagle feathers for the showdown to come. He spoke harshly to Procter: 'Your words, father, are like the smoke from our pipes, they rise in the air and vanish. You are like a crayfish, unable to walk in a straight line.' The sequence of events is not entirely clear, but he stormed out of Procter's tent and mustered his troops from many Indian nations. He was killed in the first volley. His body was never found.

✻　　✻　　✻

The objects in the medicine bag, which is of a soft skin, have decomposed, except for a migis shell like mine and the tips of miniature arrows. The dog sniffs the bag cautiously. The *Dictionary of National Biography* revealed that Alleyne had a distinguished military career, served for a time on General Procter's staff, and rose himself to the rank of Major General. He was lightly wounded at Detroit and wrote papers on ethnography, as well as collecting specimens wherever his career sent him.

Why have I stolen these things? I have stolen them because Gary Pale Eagle needs them. He loves me, however mad his purpose is.

He often speaks about you.

For him our boyhood selves, the spirit world, the Battle of Detroit, the sacred scrolls, exist all at once in one universe. And what do I want? Not much, it seems. I've given Stephanie all she asked – the papers are signed – and I have put my house on the market, in anticipation of leaner times.

I have a friend at Sotheby's, who is sending a skilled art packer to box up these things tomorrow. God knows what he will make of them, a decaying bag and a piece of bark with childish figures inscribed on it. I can make out, I believe, a buffalo and a thunderbird, as well as the tipis and ladders.

18

Stephanie has important news for me. She is surprised and gratified by my capitulation, and now she is coming to talk to me in person, because she knows there has been a lot of bitterness.

I take the dog out into the park to brace myself for whatever is to come. It's dark enough to let him off the lead without being seen by my fellow committee members, and he rushes away into a dense shrubbery of spiky bushes with holly-shaped leaves. I will be leaving this Eden soon. The estate agent tells me that property around here is selling as fast as it did ten years ago. For an agent this is good news. To me it indicates a certain crayfish quality, an inability to walk in a straight line. Maybe I am looking for imagery in the natural world now, like Gary Pale Eagle.

I circle the tennis court and the children's playground, which Stephanie would walk quickly past as though it were nodding and winking at her lewdly. I call the dog but he doesn't respond. I walk around the whole seven acres calling his name. Then I stand, listening to the evening noises of London, already thrumming and throbbing quietly, as if the turbine is slowing; to me this is a thrilling noise. The dog will come back; he knows the way. I call his name again anyway.

'Herbie, Herbie, Herbie.'

I wait a moment, hoping to hear the apologetic scuttling. I

sometimes wonder if dogs think their name is theirs alone, or whether they simply recognise a tone.

Stephanie is already standing on the doorstep writing me an angry note. I let her in.

'Where have you been? You said eight.'

'Don't you still have a key?'

'You changed the locks, remember?'

I feel again the heaviness of soul which our conversations always summoned.

'I was walking the dog. I've lost him, that's why I'm late.'

Her face, which is often unnaturally brown, sometimes even verging towards a tangerine colour, is now very white, her red mouth a vivid slash. My first thought is that she is going to tell me she is ill, this is the important news, but I soon see that it is part of a new pale look.

'What's this stuff?' she asks.

'Oh, it's some Indian antiques I'm sending to a friend in America.'

'Are you sure they're antiques? They don't look much. And they smell.'

'How are you?'

'I'm fine. I've had a bit of time and space, all the clichés, and I've got a new partner. I thought I should tell you, face to face. That's one of the reasons I came, so that you wouldn't just hear it casually.'

'Thank you. I appreciate it.'

'Do you want to know anything about him?'

'Not really. But I am sure you want to tell me, so go ahead.'

'God, you can be cruel. I'm glad I came over to remind

myself, just when I was feeling warm and grateful towards
you.'

'The house is for sale.'

'What's that supposed to mean, that I've driven you into
bankruptcy?'

'No, Stephanie, just that I have made all the concessions you
and Pete and Jacqueline wanted, so I feel I am entitled to regard
the matter as closed.'

'I don't think it can be closed, not just like that.'

'All right, I'll get you something to drink first. There's still
some of your herbal gunk left.'

I make myself busy in the kitchen. A large spoonful of Arabica
goes into the cappuccino machine and I place a Fruits of the Forest
tea-bag in a mug. When I add the water, it gives off the smells not
of the forest, but of a sachet in a country hotel, the sort of place
where we used sometimes to weekend, if they took dogs.

I don't want to know about her new partner. I don't want to
hear that her life is straightening out, that he makes love like a
billy goat, that she is keen to remain friends, after all we shared
so much; I don't want it said that everything could have been
so different if I was a little less selfish, but of course my career
gave me an inflated sense of importance, surrounded by all those
adoring women — *You were once one of them. Yes, that's how I know* —
and I don't want to hear that she loves me, if not in the old
way, certainly in a more grown-up fashion. And I don't want to
try to explain to her my new, more receptive frame of mind.

'So what have you been up to, then, in the old US of A?'
she asks as I put down the tray.

'I was a speaker at my high school reunion.'

'Was it interesting?'

'It was. Steph, say what you want to say. By the way, I think you look great.'

'I've been working out.'

'Do you get white from working out?'

'No, it's heroin chic.'

She laughs suddenly and freely and I am reminded of what I used to love. And it's something now as lost as Laughing Water, whose tresses flowed in the Indian breeze.

'It's a bit stale,' she says, sipping her tea.

'There hasn't been much demand. But anyway, my cappuccino is fine. Shoot.'

'You sound slightly American. It's nice.'

'Let's have it. I am prepared.'

'Well, for a start his name is Terence, and he's a graphic designer. He's a little younger than me, and he's starting his own studio.'

My money is going to fund this doomed enterprise.

She goes on: 'Which should be up and running in a few months. He's very kind and he wants to start a family as soon as possible. I haven't told him yet but he's already started. I went to the doctor on Monday to be sure. That's the main reason I came to see you, really, because I want our future relationship to be based on honesty. I didn't want you to find out from anybody else.'

'What's this Terence's second name?'

She pauses.

'Dobbs.'

'Not the same Terry Dobbs who worked in our design studio?'

'Yes. He went freelance.'

'He was sacked for being completely useless and unreliable. Sorry, but I just want you to know the sort of person the

226

father of your unborn infant is. A total wastrel. Anything else you would like to tell me?'

'God, you're such a shit.'

'As a matter of fact, I have discovered offspring of my own in America. A daughter, to be precise. So now we're both parents, only separately. How ironic.'

I intended to be firm with her to stave off any hope she might be harbouring of a reconciliation. But I have been far too harsh; she is in tears and the red mouth is smudged in a way that causes my heart to limp painfully.

'Stephanie, I didn't mean it. I could say I've been under a lot of strain, but that would be too easy. It's only really just sunk in. I realise that I have nothing to do with the rest of my life. What you said about the agency was right, I saw that I have been living in a false ...'

'I haven't mentioned the agency.'

'Well, what you used to say. It takes some adjusting, and that's what I suppose I was doing in America, without realising.'

She dabs her eyes on her sleeve.

'What's this family?' she says quietly.

'It's not true. At least, it's almost certainly nonsense. I just said it to get back at you. I'm delighted that you're having a baby, if that's what you want.'

Now she whispers, 'I still love you, Dan.'

I don't deserve all this love. I see that her violently red mouth is the colour of the paint Gary applied to my face when he shot me with the migis.

'Don't, Steph, you have your baby, with my blessing.'

Nobody nominated me, but I seem to have assumed a sort of godfatherly role (on two continents). I have to force myself to remember that this quivering, beautiful woman with the urgent face was trying, with my former partner, to blackmail me. Such is the strange complicity between men and women, that I believe she would be prepared to have sex now, to seal some sort of agreement.

'Dan, will you kiss me one last time?'

I kiss her, but it's nothing like the sort of kisses we once exchanged, which were wild and tender. As you get older you see kissing as more significant than fucking, even obscene, the same way prostitutes do. Your face is so intimately yours, where everything you own lives; where your life is cooped up; by contrast your sexual organs are in the outlying suburbs.

'It's not wrong, is it, to want a baby?'

'No Stephanie. It's not wrong. I am terribly, terribly sorry. In the past week I have realised how badly I behaved towards you.'

'Do you think we were wrong for each other?'

She is gulping for air between words, and her mascara is trickling down over the newly pale cheeks. I feel sick to have been the cause of misery. But I can't answer her question.

'You think I'm not good enough for you. Dan, I'm not saying that as an accusation, we're past all that, but it's the truth. Whatever your standards were, which you kept changing, I didn't quite meet them. Except the sex, of course.'

'Stephanie, don't. Don't cry.'

I hold her to me till her sobbing stops. I don't want to have this power (if indeed I do), of being instrumental in other people's happiness. It's a burden I want to lay down.

'Steph, I have learned a few things in the past week, and the most important thing I have learned is that my version of what goes on in the world is seriously faulty.'

'But you'll think it through and come up with a conclusion which is flattering to yourself, I'm sure.'

'I'll certainly try.'

I am wondering where this new perceptiveness has come from.

Stephanie has gone.

The dog has not returned. I take the keys of the garden and enter near the silent tennis court. I love to hear the sound of tennis in the distance, the thwack of the balls, the shrieks, the laughter.

I call the dog's name: 'Herbie, Herbie, Herbie, here boy,' but there is no answering rush from the bushes. Maybe there's a bitch on heat somewhere.

There are no stars — there rarely are in London — but I wonder none the less where the region of the thunderbirds is located, without expecting an answer. I sit on a bench under a giant magnolia, now coming into leaf. Only a few of the huge, pink marbled flowers are left. Above the treeline, above the white houses, there is an orange sherbet glow in the sky. I call the dog once more, without success, before going to bed to read about Tecumseh, and his efforts to rouse his people: 'Soon your mighty forest trees will be cut down to fence the land. Soon the white man's broad roads will pass over the graves of your fathers. You will be driven from your native lands as leaves before the storm.' I read the account of a Capt. Leslie Combs: 'I was near Tecumseh when he made his speech, whereby the lives of hundreds of prisoners were saved. He was a truly great man

229

and a gallant warrior.' It was near Detroit, not far from the River Rouge, that Tecumseh intervened after an Indian massacre. I sleep, but rise every hour or so until dawn to see if the dog has returned.

In the morning the gardener awakes me. He is an ex-army officer who suffered a breakdown, and he gardens wearing a tweed jacket. He is carrying a yellow garden refuse bag. He opens it and takes out the body of my dog, damp and bloodstained.

'I'm sorry, Mr Silas, we've been getting a few big dog foxes coming in at night; they come up from Holland Park. I found him just past the children's playground.'

I bury the dog in the back garden. The corpse is so small I don't need to make a wide hole, but I dig quite deep, down into the London clay.

In my readings about the Shawnee Prophet, I have learned that dogs were sacrificed – strangled or burned on a fire – then hung up and decked with ribbons to provide a link to the Great Spirit. Dog meat was offered to strangers, as a particular honour. During the Dog Dance, the liver of a dog was eaten.

I'm thinking about this when the art packer arrives. He looks at my rudimentary items.

'No problem,' he says. 'You should see some of the things I have to pack. You wouldn't believe it.'

Back in Hackney, the scene of my crimes, I discover after a few hours what I've been looking for, and knew I would find: the location of the remains of Tecumseh. In a note attached to some letters from General Harrison to General Procter about peace terms, Alleyne describes how he and another officer, a Lt Boyd, took Tecumseh's body away and buried it in the churchyard of the Mission at Moraviantown in the middle of the night. Alleyne makes it clear that he did this of his own initiative, so that the Americans would not be able to use the body for propaganda purposes:

I deemed it a small personal victory that I should deprive General Harrison of this pleasure, to be able to produce the body of this fine man, who wanted nothing more than the happiness of his people, for his own glory.

19

Today we rebury Tecumseh.

It took some time to get permission to dig up his remains. Moraviantown, where Alleyne's letter located the burial site, is in Canada across the Detroit River. There were talks between Government departments and equipment was brought in to examine what was under the deep-frozen Canadian topsoil before the grave was located with reasonable certainty. The remains of the buckskin coat Tecumseh put on after throwing away the brocaded General's jacket were found in the grave with the skeleton. Also buried with him was a medal, given to him by General Procter's more competent predecessor, and some beadwork, its pattern lost in the decay. The skull was found to have been damaged by a bullet.

A small party crossed the border, through the tunnel from Detroit at midnight to receive the remains. The Canadians would not allow any ceremony at the graveside for fear of arousing local jealousies. Apart from rival claims to the remains, the grave of Tecumseh might have been good for business. But the Canadians felt it would be politic to respect the demands of the Native American Graves Repatriation Act, to return the remains to the appropriate authorities, led by Johnny Rattling Hawk, Gary Pale Eagle's associate. It was decided that Tecumseh should be buried secretly in a place known only to the tribal authorities, where the remains could be honoured.

But this presented a difficulty, because fifteen years after Tecumseh's death his people were removed to Kansas, a heart-breaking two-year journey. His brother, Tenskwatawa, is buried under what is now Kansas City. Other traditional burial grounds have been lost to freeways and shopping malls, and his people are fatally dispersed. What was needed was a place that would never be disturbed and that was appropriate for the burial, and at the same time was not going to be exploited by local tribal groups for their own ends. As the person who established where the great man's remains were buried, I was invited to the ceremony, due to take place when a suitable resting place could be found. For a month or two the remains were under guard in a secret location. Nobody but a handful of people knew where they were.

I have talked twice in the months that have passed to Gary Pale Eagle. He has been having treatment for a mild epilepsy and the drugs have left him subdued and silent. This is Gene's diagnosis. And it is true that our telephone conversations have been difficult. He has been working on the migration chart, trying to locate every one of the places mentioned with the aid of computers. What he is doing as far as I can understand it is to work out the most likely route of the migration and then with army maps and satellite pictures to identify the thousands of places referred to by their modern names. The places are the key to understanding the traditional songs and the ancient wisdom of the scroll. The recovery of this wisdom is necessary for the rehabilitation of the Red People. I know there have been many instances of peoples coming together around some comforting myth. There are times in a people's history, usually some years ago, which seem to be more charged with meaning, times when people were more truly themselves, than they are now. You have only to think of the Children of Israel.

Those of us who have been chosen to attend the ceremony have been sworn to secrecy. We are to meet before daybreak at this hotel, from where we will be taken in a bus with darkened windows to the secret burial ground.

I am lying awake, waiting for my dawn call.

Yesterday I drove up to Bronner's Christmas Wonderland. I expected business to be slack — after all, there are seven months to go — but no, the elderlies were arriving by the busload; the Christmas spirit was fighting gamely with the spring sunshine. The only concession to the season that I could see immediately was the absence of the Christmas-tree avenue. But perhaps the Christmas figures and ornaments looked somewhat out of sorts. It was inappropriate, and possibly cruel, to ask reindeer to carry on in this muggy heat.

I have written to Gloria twice, once trying lamely to explain why I felt I had to visit Fred Larssen, and a second time asking her if there was anything that I could do for her. I have given large sums of money to Stephanie; a little more wouldn't hurt. I was also thinking of Belinda. But Gloria didn't reply. Gene said that she was fine, probably going to get married to her friend; in fact she and Karen were talking of a double wedding on Oahu, or possibly on some Caribbean island. Palm trees equal romance, I thought, remembering our Hawaiian-themed prom. Duane was a dickhead, but Karen had settled for what she could get, Gene said. The two cheerleaders were in harness

again. I felt a pang of jealousy; I heard a door closing on
me.

It hadn't occurred to me that Gloria might not be working in
Christmas tree trims any longer. I waited a few minutes, but
there was no sign of her. One of the women on the check-outs
told me that she had been promoted, and no longer worked on
the floor: she was a manager. She said I could call her office on an
internal phone.

'Dan? Where are you?'

'I'm in London.'

'Why are you calling me?'

'Because you didn't answer my letters.'

'I couldn't. To tell you the truth, I was beginning to wonder
about Larry, my friend. It seemed unfair to him. I was talking about
you all the time.'

'Larry, the one you are going to marry?'

'Maybe. Dan.'

'Yes?'

'Why are you lying to me?'

'What do you mean?'

'You are downstairs at the check-outs.'

'How do you know?'

'First off, it would be some coincidence if you were playing
exactly the same bars of "Jingle Bells" in London as we are. And
I can see you.'

'How?'

'I'm the manager of this section, trims, lights and candles. I have
TV monitors.'

'Can you come down?'

'No, Dan, but you look nice, even in black and white. Very suave.'

'Why don't you come down?'

'Because, Dan, we don't live in the same world. I'm just a broad from Hollybush, and you are . . . I don't know exactly what you are, but let's face it, you find the whole situation kinda intriguing, but that's just about the long and short of it. I don't think you care about Belinda, and I don't really blame you. For a while there I did, especially when I spoke to Gary about it and he said you had tried to speak to her. I was real grateful for that, but I realised that you were playing some sort of game, even if you didn't know it yourself.'

'Gloria, things have changed for me in the last few months.'

'And for me, Dan. Like they say, time is the great healer.'

It was a long drive back to the hotel. Gloria had had the last word. I couldn't deny that my motives were suspect, but also I was happy to hear that Gloria and her Larry, whom she had kept hidden from me, were going to marry. I hoped that the spectre of Scott Hollinger would begin to fade. Time is the great healer, true, but the process is speeded up by romantic considerations and the contemplation of weddings. I saw the double wedding under the palm trees providing, like a double date, a certain solidarity, and a friend to fall back on. It seemed to me the perfect situation for two cheerleaders, in tandem.

When Gloria accused me of duplicity, I could have told her that Fred Larssen had said how unlikely it was that I could have been the father. I could have told her what our romp in Thomas Jefferson's bed meant to me. I could have tugged at the thin wires – the iron string – that had linked us together, or more accurately which had

237

attached me to my boyhood self; I could have reproached her myself with the fact that she had told me under the fragrant dogwoods on the little mountain in Virginia that I was her first and only love. I still feel a little pain that she should have deceived me in Jefferson's groves. And then apparently she cried on the bus; perhaps the real reason was that she was thinking of Fred.

The alarm wakes me, even though I have imagined myself awake for hours. There are many sorts of sleep, some of them presentiments of death. Emerson described sleep as muzzling the dogs which had worried him during the day. I have been reading a lot of Emerson in the past months, as if I could interpret my Hollybush days that way. I dress quickly and make myself a coffee, and wait for the call which comes promptly at 5:30.

Outside a small bus is waiting, windows blackened. As I approach, the doors open. Johnny Rattling Hawk greets me. In his hair are two eagle feathers, and around his neck he wears beads and a migis shell. His face is decorated with two broad red stripes, one from the cheekbones across his nose, and the other on the line of his ears.

'Dan, welcome. We owe you our thanks. These are the representatives of all the bands who fought with Tecumseh. I would like you to meet them. And of course Gary's here too.'

I am looking for Gary. It takes a while, but then I see him sitting, head bowed at the back of the bus. His feathers are tilted forwards. His eyes, however, are directed towards me, but he seems to be unable to move. His face is spotted, red below the ears, and green up to the band of red cloth tied around his head to secure the feathers.

'Gary is not in good shape, Dan, but he wanted to come. He wanted to see you.'

He introduces me to the six men and one woman, representatives of the Ojibwa, Shawnee, Potawatomi, Chippewa, Creek, Wyandot, Kickapoo and Fox tribes. One or two of them don't look particularly Indian, but they're all dressed in feathers or beads and buckskin and most have their faces painted. They have ears decorated with pendants of fur or feathers or shells. They are silent, and shake my hand gravely. One man says, 'We thank you, sir.'

I go to the back of the bus and for a moment or two I put an arm around Gary Pale Eagle. He tries to say something, but he cannot.

'Don't worry. No need to speak,' I say.

The bus sets off. After a journey of no more than a few minutes in the dark it stops again. I can hear guarded voices. We move forward into the darkened but familiar landscape of Greenfield Village.

Gary is holding my hand. I am not certain from his tortured face what he is feeling, but I hope it is fulfilment. I peer at Henry Ford's birthplace, the Loranger Gristmill, the Miller Schoolhouse, Wright's Cycle Shop and Home; then we make a right turn past Edison's Menlo Park complex and the Sarah Jordan Boardinghouse where his first employees lodged. We pass the Edison Homestead, the George Washington Carver Memorial (a reconstruction of the slave cabin where he was born) next to the genuine slave cabins, and then we turn near the Noah Webster Home. Just beyond the Cotswold Forge, where the land rises to a small hillock overlooking the lake, we pull off. There is some light in the sky over towards Detroit, but as yet no sun.

I help Gary off the bus. In the semi-dark, as we file through the trees with our feathers and drums and prayer sticks and other sacred objects, we look like an Indian raiding party. Greenfield Village is completely silent, except for some roosting birds by the lake which begin to shriek. The first drumbeat sets them wheeling. All the party follows the drummer and Johnny Rattling Hawk, who is carrying the remains of Tecumseh in a satchel. Another man is carrying the medicine sack.

Now Johnny Rattling Hawk chants: *Manitou, i yani, manitou, mide wi he.*

He is calling to the Great Spirit, to tell him the good news that his son is returned. We chant *He-he-he-he — yo* as we march, Indian file down towards the lake.

Ka wi ka da an na we.

He-he-he-he — yo.

I see that Gary's lips are moving silently. When we reach the lake's edge, near the landing where the paddle steamer halts in summer, the sun is silvering the water and the sky above is taking colour. The burial site is in some trees, part of the ancient forest, looking down on the lake. In turn all the shamans offer prayers to the Great Spirit.

It was my suggestion to bury Tecumseh here. My researches showed that it was on this exact spot that Tecumseh spared the lives of many of General Harrison's troops in 1812, contrary to Indian custom. A small hole has been dug: the medicine bag and the satchel are lowered by Johnny Rattling Hawk into the earth and at that moment the sun strikes the trees above us. Gary stands beside me. He is shivering. I take his hand and feel the force of the emotions which are twanging and plucking at his arm.

The shamans shovel the earth in on top of the satchel, and they rearrange the twigs and fallen leaves. One man, I notice, crosses himself. Then a small post is driven into the ground above the grave. It is an inconspicuous object, red with a green band around the top, colours which will soon fade, I imagine.

20

London

This letter reaches me from the clinic in Grand Rapids where Gary is now permanently resident.

I am Pale Eagle, the son of Red Deer and Wenonah. I send you greetings.

The first people were the Red People, the Anishnabeg, and they lived on the shores of the Great Salt Water. They took to the sea in boats and they hunted the whale.

One day the migis, a seashell, rose from the cold waters and the rays of the sun were reflected on its wonderfully lustrous shell, back upon the Red People. And they basked in its light and warmth and they prospered for many moons.

But without warning the migis sank below the surface of the waves one day, and the Red People lived in darkness and in fear until the migis rose again on the river which flows from the Great Lakes; and the Red People, seeing its light to the west, followed, and they lived there for many moons. But again the migis disappeared and the villages and encampments of the Red People were visited by sickness. The tipis and lodges stood silent.

The young men were unable to hunt, death and sickness hung over the forest, and the crows feasted on the unburied dead.

Now Nijik the Otter appeared from the water. He gave the Red People a chart, prepared by the Great Spirit, to show them where to live and how to avoid sickness. And the otter led the remains of the Red People, who could barely paddle their canoes, to the shores of Lake Superior and there the Red People built a sacred lodge in accordance with Great Spirit's instructions, conveyed to them by Nijik the Otter.

And the chart showed the Red People where to erect sacred stones and posts, and how to perform the offices of the Midewewin which would keep them safe from disease and from darkness, and help them to attain wisdom. And those who wanted to attain wisdom, were told by degrees how to fast, to dream, to take steam baths, to make offerings of smoke to the East, South, West and North. And the smoke must be drawn in slowly and reverently, and it must be blown upwards to honour the Great Spirit, and downwards also, to honour Nokomis, the earth.

Ka wi ka da an na we was si nan ...

It will never fail.

Those who had attained wisdom were shown how to decorate their faces, with stripes of green and red, and where to place the spots which showed that they had been shot with the migis.

And the Red People lived happily, hunting the deer and the bison, the bear and the elk, and catching the whitefish which made the waters boil in the straits of Bow-e-ting (Sault Ste. Marie) when they passed in their season. The Otter had told the Red People that no deer may be killed while swimming, nor may a deer with a foal be killed. All the animals must be informed of the hunter's intention, because without their consent, the animals cannot be killed. After making a kill, the hunter must leave the offal for the crow, because the crow once returned a scalp from the village of an enemy. And the Otter told the Red People how to offer prayers for hunting, prayers for love, prayers for revenge, and prayers for war ... The Red People collected the syrup of the sugar maple, they harvested wild rice and green onions, and they grew tobacco. In the swamps and the bogs and the forests they found plants which they collected for medicines. And their lives were lived according to the seasons.

The Red People multiplied, and their lodges spread far along the lakes and through the forests. They were happy, and this land was utterly beautiful.

And then the White Man came, and the White Man was never satisfied. He too came from the direction of the Great Ocean, where he had arrived in boats from his own country. He brought with him whiskey and he traded whiskey for pelts to make hats. And the Red People, who had no knowledge of whiskey, began to neglect their hunting and their fields and their fishing in favour of whiskey. The White Man also brought with him many diseases which the sumac and the snakeberry and the shield fern and the heartleaf could not cure. The Mide priests could not cure them either, and some among the Red People began to doubt the power of the Mide. And in this time, people began to lose interest in the ways of their forefathers. Once again death and darkness fell in their villages and encampments. And the White Men came in ever greater numbers and they were hungry for land.

And I was a small boy then, learning the Ojibwa language and learning to make meat and to hunt and to fish. But many people all around were already saying that the White Man was going to kill all the Red People.

Then came Tecumseh, the great chief of the Shawnee. And Tecumseh travelled all up and down the frontier, speaking to the Indian peoples, and he said to them that only by uniting could they ever hope to retain their lands. And he told them to give up drinking whiskey and kill their dogs and stop beating their women. And I followed Tecumseh until the day he died abandoned by the British, and his body was stolen. Since that day the Anishnabeg have lived furtively, like frightened animals.

And now his body has been recovered and buried in holy ground and the sacred scrolls of our people have been returned. And the time has come for our people to remember the words of Tecumseh, and to remember that Nijik the Otter led us to these lands in accordance with the wishes of the Great Spirit. And Tecumseh told us that the Great Spirit said that the Americans were not his children. They are the children of the evil spirit.

The sacred scrolls tell us of the routes our forefathers took to reach this land, the songs we must sing to speak to the spirits, the places which are holy to our people and the many places which belonged to us that have been taken away. They also tell us of the forgotten ceremonies of the warpath which make the Red People strong. We must purify ourselves in accordance with these instructions and we must set out to reclaim what is ours from the Americans. We must honour the memory of Tecumseh, by taking up our war bundles.

I am Pale Eagle. I send you greetings.

*　　*　　*

Leading the Cheers

Gary has spent months working on the birchbark scroll, trying to decide where the places referred to in it are located, and what they mean. The scroll lists thousands of place names, such as Long-Sand-Bar and Fish-Spawn-River and The Place-Where-Bark-is-Obtained and Foaming-Rapids.

Gene, who e-mails me regularly now, believes it is a hopeless task, and one which is driving Gary crazy. This seems a strange choice of phrase. Gary apparently believes that he has established that the original migration most probably started near present-day Cape Cod, not far from where the *Mayflower* first made land.

Gene also tells me that Gary is no longer allowed out of the clinic, by court order. If he leaves, he will be confined in a state institution. He is suspected of the theft of articles, including bones, from various museums. Gene says that Gary wants to see me again, that he talks of me often.

At the moment I have no plans to visit him.

However, I have accepted an invitation to travel to St Thomas in the US Virgin Islands in a few weeks for the double wedding of Gloria and her Larry, and Karen and Duane. I have agreed to give Gloria away. Gloria obviously sees some symmetry in this arrangement. St Thomas was chosen because the flights are very cheap out of season and there are special wedding packages, champagne and photography included. Gloria is worried it may be something of a production line.

Although I am not proposing to see Gary, I often think of him poring over the migration scroll. I imagine that the difficulty he is having is deciding if it is a route map or some sort of allegory. Either way, I hope that the migis will rise again and shine its light on him.

*   *   *

I think of myself as having made a small migration. I have bought a flat overlooking the canal in Hackney. There are certain times – infrequent – when the light from the migis appears to strike the water of the canal, turning it to molten silver.

Ducks venture out into this lava flow, oblivious.